HIGH DESERT ELEGY

Stories & Poems

Michael G. Vail

Cholla Needles Arts & Literary Library
Joshua Tree, CA

With the exception of "Sir Paul Visits Pioneertown",
this is a work of fiction. Names, characters, places and
incidents are the products of the author's imagination
or are used fictitiously. Any resemblance to actual
events, locales or persons, living or dead, is entirely
coincidental.

The stories and poems within have appeared in:

Cholla Needles Literary Magazine from Joshua Tree
and HOWL Art & Literary Magazine, a publication of the
Copper Mountain College Foundation: "Carnival!";
"Happy Land"; "The Lost Men"; "Dan Buster's Gold";
and "The Ravens".

Thank you to Kent Wilson for the front cover
photograph from Joshua Tree, 1947

Thank you to Johnny Nagy for the title page drawing

https://www.chollaneedles.com

ISBN: 9798708166197

For Laura, who has the patience to put up with a writer.

HIGH DESERT ELEGY

On the Sunday that Maria committed suicide, the morning sun gradually ascended into the cloudless azure sky, its blinding light filling the dining room's wide picture windows. Sprawling across a prominent ridge top, the handsome house overlooked the little town of Last Chance. It huddled in the middle of the valley floor, surrounded by a vast expanse of desolation and creosote bushes.

Samuel and Sarah ignored the panorama below. They busily scurried about the kitchen, making preparations for the arrival of their brunch guests. The two couples from Echo Park were expected by noon, and there was still much to be done.

*   *   *

"This place is at the end of the world."

The lean figure slouched on the adjacent barstool. His long white hair fell in a tangle over the shoulders of his frayed denim jacket and framed his deep blue eyes, which blazed with a pagan intensity.

"To the west, the open spaces are long gone. Nature's on the run." He shifted on the stool. "But you go too far east," he warned ominously, "and you'll fall off the earth."

Samuel and Sarah glanced at one another, quickly swallowed down what was left of their gin and tonics and asked for the check from the bartender, a young man with a tattoo of the solar system on the inside of his left arm. Stepping out of the bar and its odor of old cigarettes, they paused on Last Chance's forlorn main street. Most of the storefronts were empty; some were boarded over.

"Maybe this notion of finding a desert getaway isn't such a good idea," she noted tentatively, watching her husband as the hot wind pushed her blonde hair across her forehead.

He didn't answer right away. The desert getaway was his idea.

"We'll see," he finally said.

That afternoon, a realtor took them to see the house on the ridge. It was everything they had hoped for: mid-century architecture, remodeled kitchen and bathrooms and views of what seemed the entire Mojave.

Across the unpaved road stood an old homestead cabin, well-maintained but out of place among the larger dwellings that had been constructed around it in recent years.

"A lady from Pennsylvania named Maria lives there," the realtor told them. "She has stage four pancreatic cancer--and found out assisted suicide is legal in California."

He paused for a moment as he watched them.

"She probably won't be your neighbor for very long."

*   *   *

"The German tourists think the reason the founders of this town came here was to make contact with space aliens." The strange man on the barstool glared at the couple. "Everyone's forgotten about the real pioneers. Miners who never struck it rich. And World War I veterans searching for some place to recover from the mustard gas attacks."

So Maria is only the latest to come here for something that couldn't be found any place else, Samuel thought as he and Sarah rushed to prepare the appetizer platter and heat up the quiche.

When the black Range Rover climbed the hill and stopped in the driveway, the couple left the air conditioning to greet their guests. As everyone else went inside, Samuel hesitated, staring across the road. A cluster of cars and pick-up trucks were parked in front of Maria's place.

The six of them sat together on one side of the long dining room table, facing towards the stark red hills in the distance. By the middle of the afternoon, most of the food and sparkling wine were gone.

While they stared contentedly through the windows at the wilderness, the sound of music began to fill the air.

Maria must be gone, Samuel thought. He stood, glass in hand, walked to the front door and swung it open.

A mobile sound system had been set up in front of Maria's cabin. While "Spirit In the Sky" blasted out of the speakers and echoed off the boulder-strewn hillside, a dozen friends and members of her family bobbed and weaved in a ragged half-circle, arms raised and smiles filling their faces.

"Sounds like a party," someone said when Samuel returned.

He nodded, went into the kitchen and pulled the cork from the last bottle of Champagne.

Across the road, the celebration went on past sunset. While the Range Rover backed out of the driveway and headed back down the hill through the shadows, the music drifted over the ridge top and into the crimson sky, which slowly turned ink black and then began to fill with a million stars.

MY OLD MAN

When I was a little boy, my old man had his own way of getting my attention.

One Friday afternoon, he came home from work early, unbuttoned the starched black shirt of his policeman's uniform and opened a quart of Old Granddad. I smelled the whiskey as soon as I walked into the living room. Somehow, he'd spilled some of it on the carpet in front of the sofa where he sat.

I tried to sneak past him to the narrow hallway and the bedroom I shared with my two younger brothers. But he spotted me out of the corner of his eye.

Just as he let the empty bottle fly, I slammed the hallway's pocket door closed. It crashed against the shut door with a sound like a gunshot.

A few weekends later, I wasn't so lucky. The family was having a Sabbath barbecue in the backyard. Sunday afternoons happened to be the most dangerous time to be around him. That's when he'd be nursing a major hangover, picked up the night before at the local VFW post where the drinks were cheap and plentiful.

One of my brothers had a toy car made of metal and painted bright yellow. I guess it was supposed to be a little taxi cab. I tried to wrestle it away from him--and he let out a scream that could've woke the dead.

The old man snatched up a long, narrow wooden pole he'd purchased to stake up a recently planted sapling. Raising the pole over his shoulder, he flung it violently in my direction. Everyone watched, frozen in place--including me--as it cartwheeled across the yard like a deranged helicopter blade and slammed into my forehead.

The impact knocked me backwards and I crumpled onto the patchy lawn. Barely conscious, I felt the warm blood begin to run down my temple.

"Is he dead?" said one of my brothers as he leaned over to take a good look at the nasty gash.

My mother pushed him aside, helped me to my feet and led me into the house. She and I and the old man stood before the kitchen sink as she wiped away the blood. I should have been taken to a doctor for stitches. But instead, she laid a strip of gauze over the cut and taped it tightly into place as I moaned.

While the old man remained standing alone near the sink, Mom sat me down across from her at the kitchen table.

"When you get to school tomorrow morning," she instructed firmly, staring into my eyes, "you are going to tell your teacher you fell while you were playing and banged your head on a rock."

Still feeling woozy, I looked past her to the old man. His jaw tightly set, he stared at the blank wall next to the refrigerator and shook his head. I assumed he was still angry with me--and shuddered at the thought.

In the weeks that followed, though, I noticed a change in him. He still drank as much as ever. But he was no longer mean to me. Once, he even glanced over from where he sat at the VFW post's bar and smiled crookedly in my direction. I couldn't figure out what the hell was going on. I continued to keep my distance, though. I wasn't taking any chances.

At about the same time, another man suddenly appeared in our lives. His name was Jack. Younger than the old man, he was slim and outgoing, with a goatee and a full head of jet black hair framing his handsome features. He joined us for dinner several times a week and even drove the family to Newport Beach in his new Ford station wagon for afternoons at the seaside. And he told jokes that made Mom laugh. But the old man didn't seem to think they were funny.

"Who's Jack?" I asked Mom one day.

"What do you mean?"

"Why's he always around?"

"He's a family friend," she said.

Late on a Saturday afternoon, the old man and I were at opposite ends of the sofa, watching a Dodgers-Giants game on our black and white TV. Being around him made me nervous, but we only had one TV and I loved the Dodgers. So did he. In fact, it was the only thing we had in common.

It was the top of the sixth inning, the Dodgers were way behind and he was on his fourth glass of booze when the pocket door abruptly slid open and Mom stepped into the living room. Wearing a colorful, tight-fitting dress, her red hair was combed back in a way I hadn't seen previously. She looked prettier than ever.

As she stopped before us, the old man's face dropped.

"What's this all about?" he said.

"I'm going to a movie with some girlfriends."

"Don't go." He sounded desperate. I'd never before heard that tone in his voice.

"Why shouldn't I? All you're going to do is spend the night getting sloshed. You don't need me around."

"Stay with us," he pleaded, slurring his words.

She glanced at me, but didn't say anything. While we watched, she pulled the front door open and disappeared.

The old man looked down at me.

"She's going to meet Jack," he muttered. "I'm sure of it."

Then he buried his face in his hands and began to sob.

I slipped down the hallway. My brothers were sprawled on the bedroom's floor, playing checkers.

"How's the game?" one of them asked.

"The Dodgers are getting their butts kicked."

He sat upright. "I'm going to watch some TV."

"Not right now," I said. "Dad's still in there, and he's not feeling very good."

Soon Jack disappeared from our lives as suddenly as he'd appeared. And the old man stopped drinking. It was many years later before I came to understand the connection between these two events.

To celebrate our parents' twentieth wedding anniversary, my brothers and I scraped together enough dollar bills and change to treat them to dinner at a little Italian restaurant in the old part of town. Afterwards, we returned to the house. The old man grabbed a bottle of 7-Up and we took our usual places in front of the TV while the rest of the family filed down the hallway.

Though he hadn't touched me for a long time, I still found him intimidating. So the words I uttered that night surprised even me.

"Why'd you stop drinking?" I said.

He stared at the TV screen for a few seconds before answering.

"When I first joined the department, I'd work the night shift sometimes," he began, keeping his eyes on the game. "One night, we got a call from a woman who said a Peeping Tom was hanging around her house. I recognized her name right away. She was the ex-wife of another officer."

He was still staring at the TV. "The next day, I was off. On a hunch, I asked her ex to meet me at the VFW post."

He leaned back on the sofa and glanced my way. "The guy always seemed weird to me. Very unsure of himself. Not what you expect in a cop. Anyway, we had a drink or two and I told him about the call from his ex-wife."

The old man paused and scratched at the back of his ear.

"He didn't say much at first. But he acted nervous, rubbing his hands together on the bar top. Then he picked up his glass and swallowed the rest of his Bourbon down in one gulp. That's when he turned and told me: 'Sometimes late at night, I can't sleep. So I drive over to my old house and walk around outside in the dark.' He lowered his face, like he was ashamed. 'I look through the windows,' he said, 'and remember how it used to be between her and me.'"

The old man set down the 7-Up and gazed at me.

7

"I didn't want my life to turn out like that," he said lowly.

He leaned towards me, slowly raised one hand to the side of my face and drew the tips of his fingers gently across the scar on my forehead.

I knew this was the closest thing to an apology that I'd ever get. As I watched, my eyes filled with tears, he lowered his hand and turned back to the screen.

It was the top of the ninth, and the Dodgers had a big lead.

OLDER THAN THE SUN

The article on the internet claimed scientists have discovered solid material here on earth that's older than the sun.

I re-read the article several times; twisted its words around in my mind, trying to grasp what they meant. And pondered the questions they didn't answer.

Where did this "material" come from?

What was it made of?

And how in God's name did it get here?

When the sun went down, I stayed on the porch for a while and watched the western horizon fill with a thousand shades of red. Still I considered the article. In fact, I couldn't get it out of my head. Was it the truth? Or fake news, sent for some nefarious purpose from the other side of the world?

After midnight, I got up to take a leak. Then, despite the chill in the air, I wandered outside again. The Big Dipper loomed above me, filling the ink black void of the sky.

Just as I was about to go back to bed, I noticed a glimmer of light on the empty lot across the road. It was a small fire, barely visible, flickering among the creosote and cholla. Crouching beside it seemed to be the vague outline of a kneeling figure. But I couldn't be sure if someone was really there.

"Hey," I shouted. "What are you doing?"

No one replied. And nothing moved except the low flames.

The next morning, I made my way to the opposite side of the road. The night before, someone had lit up one of those fake fireplace logs made from recycled cardboard. A bit of its singed wrapping and a large pile of ashes were all that remained.

As I stared at the ground, looking for footprints and finding none, I wondered who it was that started the fire.

Maybe a homeless man trying to stay warm.

Or maybe the Russians.

AN INDEPENDENT MAN

On the heels of the nation's big Fourth of July Bicentennial celebration, August of 1976 began with still, warm days and mild, clear nights. It was great motorcycle-riding weather--and I took full advantage of it. Temecula's gray plains and lonely oak trees...the quiet desolation of the desert that stretches beyond Twentynine Palms...Ojai's green citrus groves and neat, small-town storefronts...I visited them all during the first two weeks of the month.

But my pursuit of happiness came to an abrupt halt on August 15. A freak hurricane swept across the southern tip of Baja California. It was strong enough to push three days of rain and uncharacteristically muggy heat into the Los Angeles basin. The city received its biggest dose of rainfall in fifty-three years while my Suzuki sat under a tarp in the garage at the back of the apartment building. I spent the seventy-two hours of tropical weather sleeping under an electric fan or else sipping gin and tonics and half-heartedly glancing through the L.A. Times' classified ads.

I've been unemployed since February, which had a lot to do with the fact that my old lady left the middle of June. "You don't want a wife," she told me in a trembling voice before she stalked out the front door, a suitcase in either hand (Christmas presents from my parents) and slipped into the waiting taxi. "You want someone who'll pay the bills, now that you've quit a perfectly good job so you can ride that stupid motorcycle all day."

Anyway, the storm finally broke about three on a steamy Wednesday afternoon. I was so grateful that I immediately went out to the garage, pulled the tarp off the Suzuki and hopped onto the seat. A push on the choke lever, a couple of jabs on the kick starter and the engine rumbled to life.

The rain-slickened streets made me hesitate as the bike's two-stroke engine shook and popped impatiently. The last thing I wanted was to take a wet corner too fast and come crashing down in the middle of a busy intersection. But the sun suddenly pushed its way through the black clouds that were already blowing north.

That was all the encouragement I needed. Pulling in the clutch, I dropped the shifter into first and guided the bike slowly down the damp driveway and onto the narrow street.

Riding north to the end of Orange Grove Avenue, I quickly turned left onto Fountain (there was a sudden break in what seemed a steady stream of BMWs, Volvos, Porsches and Mercedes), made a curb-hugging right at Fairfax and, fifteen seconds later, turned left again at Sunset just as the signal changed from yellow to red.

A row of huge billboards was there to greet me, advertising the latest disaster epics and new albums by the year's big rock stars. Just as they'd been there when I first cruised Sunset with my high school buddies seven summers before.

"Look out, Hollywood!" we'd shout out the windows of my '59 Ford station wagon as we traveled up the freeway from Orange County. It was the land of hookers and movie stars, of acid and sneak previews and topless joints. Nothing very exciting ever occurred on our visits. But possibilities always seemed to hang in the air. And the possibilities were what kept us coming back.

The sequined jump suits of the rock stars on the billboards reminded me that I was wearing worn-out jeans, a dirty T-shirt and oil-splattered sneakers. The bike didn't look "Hollywood", either. Can you imagine Warren Beatty tooling around in Shampoo on a three-year-old Suzuki? Of course not. He rode a Triumph--and Triumphs, mounted by tanned, would-be Warren Beattys dressed in expensive-looking leather were what passed me on either side of the road.

Almost to the Tower Records store, I eased my hand off the bike's accelerator. On the opposite side of the street, a tall blonde in pink shorts was struggling to push an old Honda 350 up a rise. I turned around, dodging cars as I went, and pulled up behind her.

She turned and frowned at me.

"Run out of gas?" I said.

"I don't know." She sounded exasperated. "It just stopped running."

I took the handlebars and slipped onto the seat.

"Is the ignition on?" I said, eyeing the Honda's unfamiliar instrument panel.

She reached between the front forks and fumbled with the key. "It should be."

"Where's the choke?"

She shook her head, a blank look on her face. "Sorry I don't know more about it. I just bought the thing a couple of days ago."

I raised my butt and stomped on the kick starter six or seven times, until the bottom of my foot began to ache. But the Honda didn't show any signs of life.

"It was never this hard to start before," she said. "Could you give me a lift to that Honda dealer on Santa Monica Boulevard?"

"Of course," I replied, staring into her deep blue eyes.

I felt her get on the back of the Suzuki, but she seemed to make a conscious effort not to touch me. For my part, I was nervous as hell. She was beautiful. And my wife's departure hadn't done my confidence a hell of a lot of good.

"I was planning to leave for Phoenix tomorrow morning," she shouted against the wind as I retraced my path up Sunset.

"It's lucky you stalled here instead of in the middle of the desert."

I began to relax. Taking in the stares my passenger was drawing, I felt "Hollywood"--and it felt great.

Then my bike's engine started sputtering madly.

"I'm having problems, too," I told her as I pulled to the curb.

"What's wrong?"

"Only a fouled plug. I'll have it cleaned off in a couple of minutes."

She glanced up and down the Strip until she spotted a phone booth at the Arco station on the next corner.

"I'll be right back," she told me over her shoulder as she started walking up the sidewalk.

I squatted in the gutter and took out the tool bag. I've made a real impression, I told myself. This never happened to Warren Beatty.

By the time she returned, I was losing my patience with the Suzuki. I'd already scalded my fingers on the first two plugs, and they were both free of carbon. This left only the middle cylinder, which is almost impossible to reach unless you're prepared to have road grime smeared all over your arm. I didn't have a choice.

"If the dealer can't get the Honda running, I'll have to take the Greyhound bus to Arizona," she said. "But that diesel smell always makes me sick to my stomach."

"Why are you going to Phoenix?" I asked from my knees as I thrust my arm over the hot manifold.

"That's where my family lives. I've run out of money. I had work for almost two years straight. But the studios have been dead for months."

"You work in the movies?" I said, fumbling with the spark plug wrench.

"No. I'm a recording engineer."

I turned and looked up at her. She really was mesmerizing, so slim and cool.

"Ever worked with any rock groups?"

"Yup. Fleetwood Mac, Uriah Heep." She paused. "What do you do?"

I wiped my sweating brow with the back of my wrist and, I was sure, left a smudge.

"I'm between jobs, too. I used to be a marketing writer at a big insurance company down on Wilshire. But my boss was a real asshole, so I quit."

Her eyes widened. "Say, could you do me a favor?"

"Absolutely."

"I've kept a diary during the time I've been in the business. A publisher wants me to turn it into one of those tell-all memoirs. What I need, though, is an expert's opinion on how it reads."

I forgot all about that goddamn motorcycle.

"I'd be glad to read it. I am an experienced editor." I failed to add that the experience came from working on a weekly newspaper that's distributed on the streets of Orange County for free.

Suddenly a red Jaguar sedan pulled up beside us. A Warren Beatty look-alike poked his head out the window.

"Come on, honey," he urged her as he glared at me from behind his wraparound shades.

She turned my way.

"I'm really interested in doing this memoir thing with you. I'll be out of town for a couple of weeks. If you give me your phone number, I'll call you as soon as I get back."

I recited my number while she scribbled in a little white book with inky fingerprints all over its cover.

"Good luck with the bike," she said, sliding into the Jaguar.

"See you soon."

My words were drowned out as the car roared away into the traffic. It was then that I realized I'd forgotten to ask her name. Oh well, I told myself. I'll find out what it is when she calls.

That was a month and a half ago. It's the end of September now, when the smog's especially unbearable. The radio's on, and a new song is playing.

"Hollywood girl at Sunset and Vine," intoned the singer lecherously. "Hollywood girl, you've blown my mind."

Fucking rock star. Easy for you to say. That beautiful blonde never called. But my wife did, just last week. She's filing for divorce.

"I've found someone who acts like an adult," she explained, "and I'm going to marry him."

In the meantime, I've spent most of my savings. And my unemployment benefits are about to run out. There is one bright spot about this down-in-the-dumps month, though. The weather's been warm and dry--perfect riding weather.

Last Saturday I headed down the Santa Ana Freeway to Oceanside and turned inland. It's beautiful out there past Escondido. Tall eucalyptuses line the winding, narrow country roads and the bright, clear sunlight shines on everything. Guiding the Suzuki along--a push on the handlebars at this curve, a twist of the throttle as I cross an oak-shrouded ridge--brought me peace of mind.

Yeah, it's 1976, the year of the Bicentennial. And I'm an independent man.

SUMMER SOLSTICE

June 21, 1969:

The sun seemed to hang motionless in the cloudless sky above the valley. By mid-morning, the temperature had reached ninety-five and the eleven and twelve-year-old boys who had been hoeing half-heartedly at the weeds in front of the old schoolhouse were told they could leave.

"It's a good way to get the school district sued--makin' 'em work in that heat till someone faints an' falls on a rock an' cracks open his skull," Harvey muttered to himself as the boys ran down the narrow country road. They were headed for one of the irrigation canals that crisscrossed the valley; a few had already pulled their T-shirts over their heads.

He took off his straw hat and wiped his wrinkled brow and large, balding head with a soiled red bandana. Then he turned and began to retrieve the discarded hoes.

Except for the loud rumbling coming from a passing crop duster, he worked in silence through the rest of the morning. A little before noon, his wife came by to drop off the lunch sack he had forgotten that morning. He and she and the neighbor lady who drove her to the school stood beside a bed of ice plants and talked about Cesar Chavez--all three were sure he must be a Communist-

-and the fact that it was the Summer Solstice, the longest day of the year.

He didn't see another soul through the rest of the day. While the heat increased, the day's stillness raised a humming in his ears that was interrupted only by an occasional metallic scraping when his hoe found a buried stone.

As the sun finally began to descend, Harvey fumbled impatiently with the storage shed's padlock. He turned and walked through the gathering dusk to the unpaved parking lot where his beige '53 Chevy coupe waited.

At least it looks like they didn't let any air outta my tires, he told himself as he circled the car. But they was busy runnin' down to the canal.

He pushed his wire-rimmed glasses farther up on the bridge of his wide nose and steered the Chevy onto the empty road. Dim pinpoints of light, separated by citrus orchards and stretches of alfalfa or fallow fields, blinked on here and there. The incessant chirping of crickets and bits of conversation from the porches of the houses were the only sounds he could hear above the engine's rattle.

Soon he passed through a small town. Besides the trucks of several farmers who were making use of Main Street as a shortcut to someplace else, the only sign of life came from the front of the bus station. A young man in an olive colored Army uniform paced before the wooden bench with the peeling ad for a mortuary painted on it, a bulging duffle bag at his feet. He had graduated from high school with Harvey's son. The old man avoided looking his way.

The Chevy's headlights suddenly revealed a pair of blurred skid marks on the asphalt. The wide, jagged patches of burnt rubber streaked down the middle of the road for fifty feet before careening to the left, towards the outline of a dimly lit house. Harvey followed the tracks until they plunged off the road. Just past where they ended, he turned onto a short plank bridge. The car stopped in the house's front yard, next to a pick-up truck of indecipherable make and model, almost invisible in the shadows.

Harvey groaned as he slipped out from behind the steering wheel and stepped around the side of the house. Since the irrigation canals surrounded his property, the water's burbling filled the night.

Another man, slim and much younger, waited alone at the back of the building, beside a row of chicken coops. He sat in his overalls on one of two upright wooden crates that had been placed on either side of a glowing kerosene lamp.

As Harvey approached out of the darkness, Frank raised his head.

"You worked late today," he said while the old man settled slowly onto the top of the second crate.

With a grunt, Harvey bent down. Reaching between his legs, he grasped the neck of a bottle and pulled it from the inside of the box.

"Damn kids," he said, unscrewing the bottle's top. Tilting the neck towards his face, he filled his mouth with the whisky.

"What about the kids?" Frank said as he reached for the bottle.

"I had to let 'em all go! Shit, they would a' started droppin' like flies in that heat."

"You don't say. Well..." Frank's voice trailed off as the hens stirred uneasily in the coops.

"Hell of a thing--that boy runnin' his Mustang into the canal," he said after a moment.

"Sure as hell was."

Harvey produced a plug of tobacco from his shirt pocket and bit off a mouthful.

"We was lyin' in bed," he said, "just about asleep. That's when he came tearin' down the road."

He turned his head to one side and spit tobacco juice onto the ground.

"All of a sudden there was a crashin' sound like I've never heard. After that, everything got quiet. Too quiet, I thought. So I pulled on my trousers an' shoes an' grabbed my flashlight.

When I got outside, I couldn't believe what I saw--the Ford stickin' straight up an' down in the canal like a space rocket that's crashed to earth. The water was rushin' through the open windows. At first, I figured whoever'd been drivin' had got out somehow an' run off into the fields. That's when I spotted an arm flappin' around just below the waterline."

His companion shook his head. "He must a' been drunk as a skunk."

Harvey, staring wide-eyed into the lamp, didn't answer.

He must be thinkin' of Harry again, Frank told himself. He had known Harvey's son all the young man's life. Harry was easy to get to know if you liked to raise a little hell. The sheriff locked him up for drunk driving and indecent exposure the night before he was supposed to board the bus to San Diego and Marine boot camp. But there was another bus, and by then Harry was out of jail. Frank had been at the Greyhound station as Harvey shook Harry's hand and turned away, tears in his eyes, and Hilde flung her arms around her boy's neck. And Frank was there on the afternoon, eight months later, when the telegram arrived at the house, telling the elderly couple their only child had died in a Viet Cong rocket attack on Da Nang.

"You know what?" Harvey said, shifting his weight on the box. "When I was pullin' that boy outta his car, I got this crazy idea in my head that it was Harry who I was savin'."

They sat there a while longer, surrounded by the sound of the water, until Frank got to his feet.

"Guess I'll be goin'," he muttered.

After the pick-up truck rumbled across the bridge, Harvey shut off the lamp. He stayed outside in the blackness for a long time, though, drinking from the bottle. When he finally stood, he did so unsteadily.

An old woman knelt under a bare bulb that hung by a black cord from the bedroom's plaster ceiling. She was looking through a stack of photographs. Harry dressed for his first day of grammar school. Harry in his high school football uniform. Harry staring, unshaven and unsmiling, at the camera before his hut in Vietnam.

"You got those pictures out again?" Harvey said harshly, slurring his words as he stumbled into the room.

She turned her head.

"Quit sneakin' up on me!" she snapped, glaring at him.

Wordlessly, he sat on the edge of the bed and began tugging at one of his dusty boots. As he did so, he let out a long breath.

"My back's botherin' me," he said when he'd gotten the boot off.

The tiny woman squinted at him. This deepened the wrinkles that lined her face.

"You worked too long today."

She carefully placed the pictures in a shoe box full of old bills and greeting cards and pushed her long white hair back with both hands as she stood.

"Did you lock the car?" she asked wearily, as though questioning a child.

"Yeah." The second boot slipped off in his hands. When he got off the bed, she pulled the blanket back.

"You heard what the law's plannin' to do with that boy?" he said loudly from the adjacent bathroom.

"I hope they lock him up. Those guards at the county jail might be able to knock some sense into him."

"Hell, woman. He was just havin' a little fun." Harvey spoke with drunken bravado.

Hilde set her hands on her hips.

"Yeah, that was lots a' fun--almost drivin' his car into our bedroom. What'd you do with your pillow?" she said impatiently.

"It's in the Chevy. Sittin' on it makes my back feel better..."

She stalked out of the room and he heard the screen door slam shut. Hope she remembered the key, he told himself.

She hadn't. "I wish to heaven you'd think a' somebody else for a change," she said when she returned with the pillow after her second trip outside. "It's the same thing with you always forgettin' your lunch. I've got better things to do than huntin' up somebody to drive me to the schoolhouse."

They were lying in bed under the single blanket, facing the open, curtainless window. The lights of a passing car crept over their bodies and up the wall.

He pressed against her. "I'm sorry," he whispered.

She found his hand and clutched it in hers.

"I am too," she answered as her eyes filled with tears.

Meanwhile, the water in the canal rolled on past their window.

SIR PAUL VISITS PIONEERTOWN

I.

During the summer of 1968, I got a job working at a car wash and was able to save enough money to pay cash for a nine-year-old Ford station wagon. I also was invited to a neighborhood party where I met four girls, good friends who had just finished their freshman year of high school.

The girls and I spent much of the summer together. None of them had a driver's license, so my station wagon became a magic carpet that took us to the sands of Newport Beach, picnics at the county park and evenings at the drive-in theater.

One day, I surprised them with an announcement: I'd snagged five tickets to see Jimi Hendrix at the Hollywood Bowl. Our seats were in the very last row, literally at the top of the Bowl. But we didn't care. We were together, watching an amazing performance by a unique artist.

In the years since, I've attended lots of great concerts and seen some wonderful acts, including the Who, the Stones, Sly Stone, the Kinks, Bob Dylan, Led Zeppelin and Miles Davis. But nothing had ever topped that night in September, 1968. It wasn't just the music. It was the venue. And it was the companionship I felt—not only with Sherrie, Jana, Vivian and Stacey. But with everyone else at the sold-out Hollywood Bowl. We all knew we were experiencing something special together.

I never could have predicted that I'd spend an equally memorable evening with three-hundred other lucky souls in a one-time biker bar at the edge of the Mojave Desert, thrilling to the presence and performance of an equally legendary musician. But forty-eight years later, that's exactly what happened.

II.

When you settle onto a stool at Pappy & Harriet's Pioneertown Palace, the first thing you notice is an impressive sculpture perched in a place of honor behind the bar. A middle-aged man with plenty of character lines on his face stares at you from under a wide-brimmed cowboy hat and a full head of hair that falls over his shoulders. There's only one complaint I have about the authenticity of the statute. It's subject isn't smiling.

I met Pappy Allen in 1984, two years after he and Harriet purchased the joint. It was a lazy weekday afternoon. The only ones in the room were the bartender and a big man who sat alone at a table next to the vacant dance floor. He had a drink in his large hand.

"Come over here and join me," he said.

"This your bar?" I asked after the bartender delivered my bourbon on the rocks.

"Sure is. It used to be called The Cantina. Kind of a rough spot. The Hells Angels would stop in. When we bought it, I told the Angels they were still welcome. But they wouldn't be able to wear their colors." He paused and stared at me. "I want everyone to feel welcome."

I and my wife, Laura, had just had a house built on Rancho Mesa at the top of Old Woman Springs Road as it winds out of Yucca Valley. Pappy & Harriet's was an easy and scenic fifteen minute drive away through Pipes Canyon. During the next four years, we saw quite a bit of Pappy and his bar.

III.

I'd been introduced to the Morongo Basin in 1968—the same year the girls and I saw Jimi Hendrix—by a man named Al Newhart. He owned the Chevron gas station where I worked while I was in junior college. Divorced and alone, he lived in a one bedroom apartment in Yorba Linda across the street from Richard Nixon's birthplace...and waited impatiently for Friday afternoons to arrive. That's when he'd climb into his 1955 Dodge pick-up truck and drive to his cabin in Joshua Tree.

Back at the gas station, he'd tell me about the high desert's stark beauty and solitude.

"You need to visit me out there," he insisted, more than once.

When I finally took Al up on his invitation, I didn't know what to expect. Wasn't the desert a place full of nothing? I asked myself. I soon found out how wrong I was.

I drove out on one of those beautiful Spring days when the cloudless blue sky goes on forever. His little cabin was nestled among the boulders at the base of the hills on the south side of the highway, footsteps from the National Monument boundary.

After I arrived, Al led me into the late afternoon sunlight. We settled into a pair of beat-up metal chairs, a can of Olympia beer in his fist and a bottle of Coke in mine. A panorama of Joshua trees, creosote bushes, silver cholla and beavertail cactus covered with purple blooms spread before us.

At the gas station, Al always seemed tense. Now he leaned back and beamed at me.

As the sun began to set, he pointed towards a tall ridge on the opposite side of Highway 62. "That's Copper Mountain," he said. "I hear there's going to be a college built over there."

A few years after that, Al met a lady who lived a mile or so from his cabin and raised goats. They fell in love. He sold the gas station and they bought a spread in Wonder Valley.

Just as Al had introduced me to the Basin, I invited my uninitiated friends to Rancho Mesa on weekends. We'd drink beer and play horseshoes all afternoon, throw a couple of racks of ribs on my Weber barbecue and then, after dinner, head over to Pappy & Harriet's.

Even on Saturday nights, there often weren't many customers. The food wasn't so good in those days and the live entertainment usually consisted of Pappy and Harriet singing old country tunes. We knew closing time was approaching when Harriet appeared from the kitchen with a tray of freshly baked cinnamon rolls—great for soaking up the alcohol before we hit the road.

Our house on Rancho Mesa had been built over a former drainage swale. The contractor didn't bother to compact the fill according to code. After four years, a large crack appeared in the foundation; it ran from the front door through the living room. The garage began to pull away from the rest of the house. I convinced the contractor that it would be best for everyone involved if he bought the damaged building back from me.

For the next twenty-six years, we got out to the high desert and Pappy & Harriet's only occasionally. Meanwhile, Pappy passed away and new owners took over.

Six years ago, Laura and I decided to return to the Basin. We fell in love with an old homestead cabin on Canyon Road in Twentynine Palms that had been expanded and remodeled over the years. And we became regulars again at Pappy & Harriet's.

We missed Pappy's welcoming smile and Harriet's cinnamon rolls. But appreciated the fact that the rest of the grub was much improved—first-class barbecue, cooked on a Santa Maria-style grill on the back patio—and the musical entertainment now included well-known recording artists.

IV.

On the morning of Thursday, October 13, 2016, Laura and I were driving back to Twentynine Palms after picking up a piece of furniture at one of the shops along Highway 62. We had dinner reservations for that Saturday at Pappy & Harriet's and decided to call and confirm.

The recorded message on the other end of the line sounded like nothing I'd ever heard before.

"Yes—it's true!" exclaimed a woman's breathless voice. "Paul McCartney will be at Pappy and Harriet's tonight!"

I continued to listen as she recited the ground rules for getting into this once-in-a-lifetime show.

"Don't line up before 3 p.m.," she insisted, "and bring cash. Admission is fifty dollars."

I turned my wide eyes to Laura, who was driving.

"We've gotta try and get into that concert!"

She shook her head. "Not me," she said. "The place'll be packed. And you know how low the stage is. I wouldn't be able to see a thing."

Laura is barely five feet tall. She was right about the stage—it's really no stage at all. I reluctantly agreed that she might find it a frustrating evening.

"Do you mind if I head up there?" I asked.

"Hell, no—go for it."

After I'd unloaded the furniture in Twentynine Palms and Laura wished me luck, I drove to Pioneertown as quickly as I could.

As I approached Pappy & Harriet's, it was high noon. The building and adjacent property was surrounded by yellow tape and security guards. Even though the phone message warned that line-ups wouldn't be allowed before 3 p.m., a group of thirty fans had assembled to the east of the security zone. I parked and joined them.

For the next three hours, the line that wasn't supposed to exist grew longer. Meanwhile, a second line formed on the west side of the roadhouse. And Pioneertown Road became jammed with vehicles as word spread about the concert throughout the Basin and the rest of Southern California.

When 3 p.m. arrived, the rent-a-cops took down the yellow tape—and all hell broke loose. The hundreds of music lovers in both lines sprinted for Pappy's entrance, intent on getting in the front of the "official" line that was forming there. Suddenly, dozens more who'd concealed themselves among the houses to the south raced across the road and joined the melee.

Once I reached the new line, I realized I was among the forty or so fans at the front. For the first time, I felt pretty sure that I was going to get inside. Those around me had reached the same conclusion. A feeling of euphoria spread among us.

"This is a fucking dream come true," said the guy standing beside me, a wide smile crossing his face. I guessed that, like me, he was old enough to have seen the Beatles on the Ed Sullivan Show.

"Yeah," I agreed, giving him a firm 'bro' handshake. "It sure the fuck is."

I turned to look behind us. The line stretched north past the Pioneertown Motel and continued on for as far as the eye could see.

V.

A few minutes later, a tiny man with salt-and-pepper hair, dressed in an expensive-looking black leisure suit and a matching visored cap, appeared with a group of burly bodyguards. He began moving down the line, stopping to make the same presentation to several dozen of us at a time.

"I'm Sir Paul's international tour manager," he explained in an upper-class British accent. He welcomed us—a nice touch!—and went over several pieces of information, including a reminder that admission was fifty dollars, cash only.

"How many can see the show?" someone asked.

"The fire department will only allow three-hundred," he replied. Then he looked past us at the rest of the line. Later, I heard that over a thousand fans were turned away.

At 5 p.m., Pappy & Harriet's front door opened and the line began moving forward. When I handed over my fifty bucks and entered, the place was almost empty. All the furniture had been moved out; it would be standing room only.

If I'd walked directly to the front of the stage, I could've been face-to-face with Paul for the entire evening. But instead, I stopped to purchase a T-shirt, poster and cocktail. When I finally staked out a spot for the concert, I was about thirty feet from the stage.

As the room filled up, the strangers who surrounded me instantly became friends. We were sharing this unbelievable experience, a night that none of us would ever forget. As I sipped on my Manhattan, I thought about the fact that Sir Paul is not only an all-time great songwriter and musician, but also one of the most famous people on earth. And I was about to see him perform at Pappy & Harriet's. It was all too surreal.

VI.

Paul and the members of his touring band took the stage at 8 p.m.

"This is the biggest gig we've ever played!" he quipped.

Then the music began. During the next hour and a half, Paul performed twenty-two songs that touched on every part of his stellar career: "A Hard Day's Night"; "Can't Buy Me Love"; "Lady Madonna"; "Hey Jude"; "Band On the Run". The hits just kept on coming.

As everyone knows, Paul has personality to spare. Throughout the evening, he was the perfect host.

"We thought it would be a nice idea to just come out to a little roadhouse like this," he said. At another point, he asked: "How many of you live in Pioneertown?" When most of the audience cheered in reply, he beamed from the stage. "That's great! We wanted to have a show for the local folks."

Later, he paused and glanced over at the bartenders, who kneeled on top of the bar to see over the crowd.

"Hello, ladies!" he shouted, waving happily.

His last number was "I Saw Her Standing There." Then he and the band were gone.

THE DREAM CATCHER

I didn't notice the neighbors when we first moved in. But that was before my boss at the advertising agency stopped at my cubicle with some bad news.

"We've lost our biggest account," he said. "I'm going to have to let you go."

With plenty of time on my hands, I'd sit at the front window of our apartment after my wife left for work, smoke a joint or two and watch the gloomy-looking two story building across the street.

The neighbors who lived there stuck to a daily routine. About 10:30, the man appeared, wearing nothing but shorts and flip-flops. Looking fifty years old or so, he was tall and slim, with just the beginning of a paunch. He paused at the doorway of his first floor apartment, yawning and stretching his long arms into the West Hollywood sunshine.

Disappearing back inside, he reappeared a moment later carrying a camp table and three folding metal chairs. These he arranged on a narrow patch of grass. The next time he emerged, he was gripping a yellow stick with a red golf flag mounted at one end, a dirty golf ball, and a putter with a rusted head and shaft.

Like an Aztec warrior slaying an unlucky Spaniard, he raised the stick above his head with both hands and drove it into the turf.

When he appeared again, he carried a jug of Gallo Burgundy and three large plastic cups. Carefully placing the cups on the rickety table's surface, he filled each one to the brim.

Pleased with what he'd accomplished, the man sat in one of the chairs, grasped a cup and took a long swig.

He invited whoever came along the sidewalk to join him at the table. They were folks with time on their hands: college students, retirees out for a walk, and the jobless, returning from the State unemployment office a few blocks away. Those who accepted his offer inevitably stayed for hours, sipping the wine and taking their turn striking at the golf ball. Whoever finally drove it against the base of the stick was the winner--and the plastic cups were refilled in celebration.

In the midst of this fun and games, an attractive redhead would suddenly step out of the apartment. She wore nothing but a towel, pinned tightly around her voluptuous torso. Girlishly, she grasped her boyfriend's arm and stood on her toes as he bent over to accept her kiss on the cheek. Then she moved to the visitor. She wrapped her arms around him if they'd met before, or shook his hand if he was a stranger. Finally, she took the empty chair and began to sip daintily from the cup in front of her.

The three of them worked on the wine and their putting skills for the rest of the day. By late afternoon, they'd gone through several jugs of the Gallo. At this point, the man and woman stood unsteadily, graciously said their farewells and disappeared into the apartment.

One morning, it was half past eleven but not a soul had come along yet to sit with the man. As I watched him, drinking alone, I decided to cross the narrow street and keep him company. It seemed like the neighborly thing to do.

While I approached, he turned his large head and stood.

"I wondered when you'd finally come over and introduce yourself." He spoke in a loud, welcoming tone.

"I'm Pat," I said.

"Ah, a fellow Irishman!"

He pulled what looked like a business card from a pocket of the shorts.

DUFFY LIVES is all it said.

While I stared at the card, he handed me a cup of wine.

"To the Irish," he proclaimed, "and whoever it was that made this wonderful juice."

A little while later, the redhead appeared.

"Oh, a new guest!" she observed coquettishly, taking my hand. "I'm Misty," she cooed.

As I'd noticed from across the street, she was quite attractive, with high cheekbones and deep hazel eyes. They were framed by her freckles and long, wavy auburn hair. But there was also something about her, something I couldn't quite put my finger on, that told me she'd traveled a few rough miles in her time. The midday sun as it filled her face revealed what my grandmother used to call "worry lines."

While we hit the golf ball and drank the wine, Duffy told me he constructed stage sets at one of the movie studios.

"When I'm hard up for cash," he added.

Misty grinned at me.

"We're winos," she announced. "That takes up most of our time."

*   *   *

I began spending a good part of most weekdays with Duffy and Misty. The only interruptions to this regimen were on the occasions when I put on one of my now neglected business suits and attended a job interview. But those occasions were few and far between. Apparently, there was an excess of copy writers in L.A. County.

Even though she was gone at her job with the telecommunications company most of the day, June began to realize how often I was hanging out with my new friends.

"Isn't there something else you could be doing with your time besides drinking with those deadbeats?" she asked one evening over dinner.

"They're not exactly deadbeats. Duffy works in the movie industry."

She stared at me and frowned.

"And what industry is Misty in?" She arched her eyebrows as she spoke.

"They're good folks. You'd see that if you got to know them."

Somehow, I convinced her that we should invite the neighbors over for dinner. When they arrived a few nights later, Duffy had slipped on a Grateful Dead T-shirt and Misty wore a pastel mini dress.

I opened a bottle of Zinfandel and poured everyone a glass. I could see that June was trying to be a good sport... although she kept throwing sidelong glances at Misty's bare legs as she lounged next to Duffy on the sofa.

We'd just finished off a second bottle by the time dinner was ready. There was barely room for the four of us around the tiny round table. As we cut into our Salisbury steaks, I mentioned that my birthday was the following week.

"How old will you be?" asked Duffy.

"Wait," Misty interrupted. "Let me guess."

She stared into my eyes.

"Twenty-three. Am I right?"

"You're right," June answered, nodding her head.

"Duffy's birthday's next month," Misty said. "Any guesses on his age?"

June pointed her finger at him--something she only did when she'd had too much to drink.

"Fifty-two," she said confidently.

Misty squealed in response.

"You're way off," she laughed.

June and I glanced at one another.

"So, how old will you be?" I said.

He paused before responding.

"Sixty-two."

"You missed it by a whole decade!" Misty exclaimed. "But I'll give you another chance. How old am I?"

Careful, careful, I thought.

June squinted at her.

"Forty-five," she answered.

Misty pressed her full lips tightly together.

"I'm thirty-two."

For a long moment, there was silence in the room as Misty stared forlornly at June. Then she covered her sad eyes with her hands and began to sob uncontrollably.

While the rest of us watched, she pushed her chair away from the table, got to her feet and rushed out of the apartment.

Wordlessly, Duffy stood and followed her.

*   *   *

The next morning, I joined Duffy as usual. He didn't mention the dinner or what had happened. In fact, neither of us said much as we drank the wine and poked at the golf ball.

At midday, Misty didn't make her usual appearance. But a very old man wearing a blue beret on his bald head came into sight, walking slowly towards us. With the aid of a polished maple cane, he moved along the sidewalk until he reached the table where we sat.

"Sal," Duffy said in greeting, "have a seat."

"Isn't that Misty's chair?" He spoke so softly that it was difficult to make out his words.

"She's under the weather today. Have a seat," Duffy repeated. "I'll go see how she's feeling."

While he disappeared into the apartment, Sal settled in and turned to me.

"You new around here?"

I nodded.

"I've been here a long time." He glanced towards Duffy's apartment. "I can remember when that building was constructed. It was right after World War II ended."

"I hope Misty's all right," he said. "Duffy's very fond of her, you know."

He leaned towards me. "She's an orphan. Passed around from one foster family to another as she was growing up." He paused. "Several of her so-called foster fathers sexually abused her.

34

"Before Duffy took her in, she was a prostitute and a heroin addict." He sighed. "She's had an unhappy life. Thank God they met."

Sal shifted in the chair.

"Know what a dream catcher is?"

I hesitated. That's a strange question, I thought.

"Isn't it a wooden hoop covered in a net or web--part of the belief system of the Lakota and other Native American tribes?"

"That's right. Duffy had been given one the studio used years before in a Western film. He hung it on the wall above their bed to trap her bad dreams. When the dawn comes, the captured dreams are supposedly destroyed by the sunlight of the new day."

He shook his head. "If only life was so simple."

"It sounds to me like Duffy is her dream catcher," I said.

*   *   *

As it happened, that was the last afternoon I spent with Duffy. The next day, an advertising agency in Newport Beach offered me a copy writer position; within a week, June and I had moved to Orange County.

About a year later, the agency's owner walked into the open office where I and the rest of the writers sat in front of our terminals.

"A new account in L.A. needs to see a piece of collateral ASAP," he announced to no one in particular. "I can't drive it up there today. Which one of you hotshots has got the time to review it with them?"

"I can do it," I said.

When the meeting with the client ended, I raced down Wilshire Boulevard, turned up Fairfax, made a right on Santa Monica and swung left through the traffic onto Orange Grove Avenue.

As I approached Duffy's apartment, I couldn't believe what I saw. The gloomy-looking building was gone. In its place on the empty lot stood a large wooden sign that announced the upcoming construction of a twenty story condo project.

That night, I dreamed about Misty.

Somehow, Duffy had died in an accident at the movie studio. Alone now, she was living on the street and dumpster diving in the alleys at the rear of supermarkets in order to find something to eat. A shadowy, featureless figure found her in one of the dumpsters, savagely grasped her slender neck and strangled her to death.

I jerked my head up from the pillow and shuddered, shaking the mattress. Breathing heavily, I pulled my hand across my forehead. It was covered with sweat.

June turned to me in the dark.

"What's wrong, honey?"

"I had a bad dream," I muttered. I lowered my face and kissed her on the forehead.

After I was sure that she'd gone back to sleep, I slipped out of bed and quietly slid open a glass door that led outside to the apartment's east-facing patio. I stood there, staring into the darkness in the cold, until the crimson glow of the coming dawn filled the horizon.

LOST AND FOUND

January 2, 1969

Elijah could still feel the chill in his bones from the howling wind outside as he stood beside the clicking wire service machine. The morning news reports from the rest of the world were about war and social unrest and cultural revolution--taboo subjects at the Pettigrew Herald.

"There's one thing you don't want to ever forget," the newspaper's circulation manager told him during his first week on the job. "What readers like in these parts is good news."

As he wound the computer tapes, he thought of Leslie. He'd call her as soon as he was off deadline. Maybe they could get together for lunch.

He'd met her two nights before at a New Year's Eve party put together by the owner of the local Ford dealership. She'd told him she was the town's librarian.

"But I'm planning to change careers soon and become a free-lance writer," she said.

"What are you going to write about?"

"People. You know, personality profiles. Human interest stories. That's why I'm moving to California." Suddenly she raised her voice. "Hippies, poets, actors, rock stars--there's all kinds of interesting folks out west!" she exclaimed.

Before going on, she glanced about her at the other partygoers. "Who's there to write about in Pettigrew?" she observed disdainfully under her breath.

He studied her pug nose and the freckles that covered her cheeks.

"I'd like to see you again."

"Got a pen? I'll give you the number at the library."

Abruptly, his daydream about Leslie was interrupted by a tapping on his shoulder. He turned to face Karl Kline, the Herald's publisher. A former Marine officer, Kline had put on quite a few pounds since his final tour of duty in Vietnam ended two years before. With his squat nose, large ears and beady eyes, he didn't wear the extra weight well.

"Have a minute?" Kline asked brusquely.

The young man didn't, but he nodded.

The publisher silently led him to his office at the front of the building. After they were both seated, Kline leaned across his large oak desk.

"What happened to the front page on New Year's Eve? The layout was a mess."

"A machine in the pressroom broke down. I couldn't use any thirty, thirty-six, forty-two or forty-eight point heads."

The older man grunted. As usual, he had no idea what went on with the paper's day-to-day operations. His only concern seemed to be the amount of advertising space sold for each edition.

"There's something else we need to talk over," he said. "A long-time subscriber called. Someone in the newsroom was very rude to her. This is the kind of thing we can't allow. I want you to find out who was responsible."

"I already know who's responsible," Elijah said. "It's me."

"You?"

"That's right. Her grandson's on the high school basketball team. She was upset because we misspelled his last name in our story about the Christmas tournament. I tried to explain I was on deadline and didn't have time to talk. But she wouldn't listen. So I hung up on her."

Kline shook his head. "That's a hell of a way for the editor-in-chief to treat our readers. What's wrong with you?"

Without warning, Elijah jumped to his feet.

"I'll tell you what's wrong!" he shouted at the startled man. "I'm overworked and underpaid, and I've had it up to her with you and the yokels in the pressroom. As for that senile old bitch, YOU can talk to her the next time she calls. Because I'll be long gone."

While Kline watched, open-mouthed with surprise, he stomped from the room and out to the parking lot and his beat-up VW bug.

When Leslie arrived for work, he was waiting on the library's front steps.

"What are you doing here?" she said. "Aren't you supposed to be writing headlines or something?"

Elijah pulled his coat more tightly across his shoulders.

"I quit my job."

She stared at him, a look of curiosity on her face, as the freezing wind pushed her curly hair to one side of her forehead.

"When were you thinking of going to California?" As he spoke, he took her gloved hand in his.

Leslie's hazel eyes widened. "Why...I don't know," she stuttered.

"I'm ready whenever you are."

A sly smile crossed her lips. "Today's as good a day as any, isn't it?"

"So what are we waiting for?" he said. "Let's pack our stuff and let our landlords know we're moving. We could be on our way before noon." He began to lead her towards the VW and her yellow Toyota sedan.

After a few steps, she stopped in her tracks.

"This is crazy, Elijah." She pulled her hand free. "I don't even know you. I can't drive off into the sunrise with a guy I just met."

He shivered in the wind. "You're right." He spoke so softly that she could barely hear him. "This is crazy."

Turning his back on her, he started walking towards the VW.

"Elijah," she called.

He glanced back at her.

"How about dinner tonight? I get off at four-thirty."

"Why not," he said, as if to himself.

*   *   *

He drove back to the newspaper office, apologized to Kline and asked to have his job back.

"All right." The publisher rubbed his large hands together like a villain in a melodrama. "But I'm cutting your salary ten dollars a week."

Elijah had been afraid that Kline wouldn't give him another chance. What other job could he get in the little town? Compared to being unemployed, the challenges at the newspaper—the tight daily deadlines, dealing with the yahoos in the pressroom and even working for Kline--seemed like small potatoes now.

At four twenty-five that afternoon, he drove by the library but didn't stop. Several miles outside town, he came upon a small bar alongside the road. The place was empty except for the bartender, a short, balding man in his late fifties who jerked his head up nervously from the Herald's sports page when Elijah walked through the door.

He settled onto a stool and ordered a Long Island ice tea.

"What's your name?" Elijah said.

"Jamie."

"Jamie what?"

The bartender stared at him. "Just Jamie."

Halfway through his second cocktail, Elijah asked: "Ever been to California?"

"Once, nine or ten years ago." He frowned. "Didn't like it."

"Why?"

"Too many people. Give me the simple life."

Elijah guffawed and slapped his open palm on the bar top while the puzzled bartender watched.

It was seven-thirty when he finally paid his bill, gingerly slipped off the barstool and stepped outside to the gravel-covered parking lot. The wind had dropped to a whisper. Several tentative snowflakes drifted in front of his face as he approached the VW.

It was then that he noticed a pair of headlights in the distance; soon the car turned into the parking lot. Suddenly Leslie was standing beside him.

"Go away," he muttered.

"I still haven't eaten," she said, affecting a tone of anticipation. "I've been too busy looking for you."

She took his hand and led him to her car.

"What do you feel like?" she said, steering the Toyota back onto the empty road.

"I don't care. Every place is probably closed now anyway."

"I bet the coffee shop near the library is still open."

The town was shrouded in blackness as they traveled down its main street. But then the coffee shop's lights appeared ahead and he followed her through the glass door to a table.

She peered at him over the top of her menu.

"How about fried chicken? It's the special tonight."

Instead of answering, he stared at the salt and pepper shakers in the middle of the table, hoping against hope that concentrating on them would stop his head from spinning.

When the waitress asked if they were ready to order, he raised his head. She was at least seventy years old, with white hair trimmed well above the blue shoulders of her uniform. There was something familiar about her voice.

"Your grandson's on the basketball team, isn't he?" he said.

She lowered her pad.

"Why, yes." A proud smile crossed her wrinkled features. "He was the top scorer in last Friday's game. They only lost the tournament championship by four points."

"If the defense had done its job," Elijah said, "your grandson's baskets would've won the title for Pettigrew."

The waitress glowed with satisfaction. "Were you there?"

"No. But I've heard plenty about it."

Her smile grew even wider.

After she walked back to the kitchen with their orders, Leslie tilted her head forward.

"How in the world do you know her?" she said.

He took her hand. "I'm glad you found me," he said, staring into her eyes.

A bittersweet feeling, of possibilities lost, tugged at her. If she had left with him that morning, they'd probably be in Oklahoma or Texas by now. But it was taking too much of a chance. Maybe later, after she was sure that she loved him.

She grinned. "I'm glad too," she said.

ALONE

The sun had not yet risen above the boulder-strewn ridgeline. Yet its glow was already bright enough to fill the window frame. The young man who lay nude on top of the bed's rumpled sheet turned his head and stared into the ethereal light. He had been awake for some time, waiting for the coming of the dawn. Now he raised his long, slim body and stretched his legs until his bare feet rested on the cracked concrete floor.

Abe's straight black hair fell over his shoulders as he stood and moved to the open window. A barren landscape of rocks and sand spread before him, its monotony interrupted only by an occasional stunted cactus or willowy creosote bush. This blanket of brown and gray rolled away from the window and across the flatlands to the base of the stubborn hills. The faint, despairing call of a quail, invisible behind a distant cholla, was the only sound that broke the leaden silence.

Knowing that the morning's relative coolness would not last long, he picked up his ripped jeans, a wrinkled t-shirt and a pair of paint-splattered canvas shoes, all carelessly discarded the night before. When he finished dressing, he stepped through an open doorway that led to the rest of the house.

This second room was not much larger than the bedroom. A toilet squatted in plain sight in one corner. In an opposite corner, a rusty refrigerator hummed loudly next to a metal sink, an old oven and a counter with several drawers. To his left as he paused in the doorway, a dining table and three plastic chairs huddled before a large window.

Beside the table was an exterior door. He grasped the knob, pulled it open and stepped outside. A sliver of blinding light had just appeared above the hilltop. Lowering his eyes, he began to wander slowly amid the sparse, otherworldly vegetation.

Other quail were calling now, and a pair of cactus wren began to clack their long, narrow beaks at the sunlight. Moving into the open desert, Abe studied the ground at his feet. His grandmother was Hopi, and he believed her DNA gave him a knack for identifying the signs of the desert's creatures.

Soon, he came upon a trail of multiple dog-like prints.

"Coyotes," he muttered, squinting at the tracks. "Five or six of them."

Stepping carefully between the antelope squirrels' burrows, he reached a dry wash where the sand thickened. A snake had passed here, leaving behind a twisting crease. He knew it had come by on the previous afternoon; this morning's sun wasn't hot enough yet to get a reptile moving.

Suddenly he stopped. Just past the snake's mark was something he hadn't seen on the property since a drunk driver killed his parents two years before. Outlined in the fine sand was someone else's footprint.

He set his jaw as he stared at the boot's mark. Raising his eyes, he turned his head and looked about him. Except for the house, now two-hundred feet behind him, there was nothing but the desert and the hills and the sun.

Abe turned back to the print. Whoever left it had been walking towards the house. Pressing his own shoe down next to it produced a silhouette that was almost identical.

It's a man, he thought.

The sand made it easy for him to follow the intruder's trail. At first, the prints continued west. But as they approached the dwelling, the tracks turned south. Following them, Abe circled the house. The trail ended in front of the bedroom window.

"What the fuck!" he muttered. The night before, someone had been standing in the dark, watching him while he stripped.

He gazed at the ground around his feet. There were no other prints beyond those that led to the window. Where did the bastard go? he asked himself, studying the unmarked sand.

His grandmother would have blamed all of this on one of the Hopi's many trickster deities. When he was a boy, before his parents decided to move to California, she'd tell him tales of how they liked nothing better than using their supernatural powers to bedevil unfortunate members of the human race.

But he didn't believe the stories then--and didn't believe them now.

"Whoever he is," Abe whispered, "he's flesh and blood."

Just after the sun set over the valley, Abe switched on the lamp next to the bed, walked out of the house and headed south. He hunkered down behind a creosote bush. When the full moon rose later that night, he would need concealment. His hiding place provided an unobstructed view of the lamp's glow as it illuminated the darkness outside the window.

Soon the sunlight faded and disappeared. Everything was black except at the window. He watched as the stars began to materialize; in no time, they filled the sky. The International Space Station suddenly came into sight, a tiny quilt of lights to the northwest. His eyes traced the station's path high above his head while he imagined being one of the crew members.

Just as the station disappeared, the full moon began to rise over his shoulder. Its muted light swept across the desert, giving the landscape a strange, dreamlike quality.

For three hours, he squatted behind the bush. The desert was quiet; all he heard was the distant howl of a lone coyote, searching for companionship, and the methodical hooting of a great horned owl.

Finally he got to his feet and walked back to the house. When he closed the front door behind him, he didn't lock it.

Standing before the lamplight, he pulled the t-shirt over his head, kicked off his shoes and stepped out of the jeans.

"Don't be shy, you son-of-a-bitch," he shouted at the window frame. "Come on in. I can't wait to get my hands on you."

When no one answered, he shut off the lamp, lay down on the mattress and listened as a wind began to blow his way from the west.

GOOD FRIDAY

As Good Friday dawned, George boarded the flight to Northern California. Until three years ago, he'd always completed this annual getaway with his wife. But since then, he had made the trip alone.

Once the plane landed in Oakland, he drove the rental car north through the density and congestion of the East Bay's cities. Soon, the highway crossed San Pablo Bay and rows of grape vines began to surround him, stretching across the flatlands and up the distant hillsides.

He pulled off in Healdsburg and steered past the town square to a little coffee shop. The place served the best BLT sandwich he and his wife had ever tasted. She wasn't normally a fan of bacon and mayonnaise. "That sandwich is flat-out unhealthy," she'd say. "But it's SO good!"

After finishing lunch, he considered taking a detour to a nearby valley where several of their favorite wine tasting rooms nestled along a pretty country road. Without her, though, this side trip didn't sound like any fun. Instead, he got back on the highway and kept driving north.

As he approached the Mendocino County line, George turned onto a two lane byway. Almost immediately, it began to climb a range of hills, zigzagging up the sides of grades and ridges; some of the switchbacks were so tight that he had to slow the car to a crawl to turn through them.

When he reached the peak of the tallest hill, the road began to descend into a pastoral valley. A hundred years before, his wife's ancestors were the first settlers to reach this remote area. In the decades since, the family had dominated its economic and political life.

In a few more miles, he entered a small town—nothing more than a dozen storefronts and a wood frame two story hotel. His wife's family had invited him to spend the holiday on their ranch just outside of the town. "Your bedroom's ready, like it's been every Easter weekend for the last twenty years," his mother-in-law told him over the phone. But this year, he chose to take a room at the hotel.

Once he checked in, George lugged his overnight bag up a flight of stairs, dropped it on the bed in his room and returned to the first floor. Because of the holiday, the hotel was full of out-of-towners. Walking back through the spacious lobby, he glanced at the bar, tucked in a corner of the room. Most of the stools were already occupied. Continuing outside to the gravel parking lot, he slipped into the rental car and pulled back onto the road.

Stands of oaks alternated with open vistas and an occasional dairy farm. Soon he spotted an unmarked dirt road. He followed it up a hill until he pulled into an overgrown clearing. Ahead of him was a clump of trees. Despite the shadows their branches and leaves threw on the ground, he could make out the shapes of the headstones, clustered among the thick trunks.

He moved slowly between the graves. The oldest markers were closest to the car. The nineteenth century turned into the twentieth under his feet as he continued walking up the rise.

His wife's plot was at the cemetery's edge, bordering a meadow of tall grass and wildflowers. There were blooms of purple, orange and yellow all around her. Next to the headstone, he rested his weight on one knee. All the marker said was her name and the words MY LOVE.

He felt her presence whenever he visited the grave. He reached down, set his open palm on the mound of soil and closed his eyes. In the clear blue sky above, a pair of ravens called to one another as they glided over the valley.

Night had fallen when he pulled back into the hotel's crowded lot. He had to circle it several times before another car backed out of a space and he could park. Now there was standing room only at the lobby bar. But as he approached, someone got off a stool and he grabbed it.

The jukebox was playing George Jones, singing "You're Still On My Mind." Next to him, a woman in her fifties with hair that was too red to be natural was telling the bartender how much she liked the way he'd made her Sazerac.

"This is just as good as the ones in Nola," she said, holding up her half-empty glass so he wouldn't miss her meaning.

"Let me try one of those," George said.

She turned to him.

"Have you been to New Orleans?" She was wearing quite a bit of make-up, all expertly applied.

"No. But it's on my bucket list."

"If you appreciate a good cocktail, you'd love it."

"Sounds like my kind of town. What's brought you to the valley?"

She pursed her lips, smudging her lipstick.

"I'm on the way to our beach house in Albion. My husband came up last week." She paused as she stared at him. "He's waiting for me."

"That's only a half hour away," he said. "Why'd you stop here?"

She continued to study his features.

"Because I was thirsty. It's a long drive from San Francisco."

His Sazerac arrived and he took a sip.

"What do you think?" she said.

"It's delicious. And strong."

She tilted her head to one side. "A little goes a long way."

He nodded. "No need to call it that fancy name. Just order 'The Painkiller'."

A wide smile crossed her face.

It wasn't long before they ordered another round.

"Are you a local?" she said.

He shook his head.

"So why are you out here in the middle of nowhere?"

"Maybe I'm on my way to Albion, too."

She grinned at him.

"You're a smart ass. I like that."

By the time they finished their third drink, the crowd at the bar had thinned out.

She stared silently at him for a moment.

"What are we going to do now?" she said.

He leaned towards her.

"Let's get another round and go up to my room."

He felt her hand in his lap.

"I like a man who knows what he wants," she whispered into his ear.

DANCE OF THE RATTLERS

The sun was low on the western horizon when he happened to glance outside and noticed something unusual in the gathering shadows. What appeared at first to be coils of thick rope filled a round clay pot that rested on the sand just below the bedroom window. As he stared at the pot, he realized the coils were slowly writhing.

"That's no rope," he whispered to himself.

Even in the twilight, he now made out a pair of triangular-shaped heads and, at the end of one of the coils, a long, ivory colored rattle.

"It's supposed to be hot today. Watch out for rattlesnakes," his wife had warned that morning before she kissed him and left for the Palm Springs airport on a flight to visit her sister in Minneapolis.

He'd seen mating rattlers on their property before. For all he knew, this might be the same pair. As he stared at the jumble of tan skin, the enfolding darkness slowly concealed the reptiles from his sight.

It was a half hour later when his cellphone rang.

"Hello," he said.

At first, there was nothing but silence on the line. He was about to hang up when she spoke.

"Remember me?"

A chill ran up his spine.

"That's a silly question." He paused. "It's been a while, though, hasn't it?"

She let out a short, nervous giggle.

"Yes, it has. How are you?"

"Okay. I'm still with the Congressman."

"I know. I read your quote on the internet last week after his desert protection bill was signed by the President."

"The environmentalists had us over a barrel," he said. "Especially with the election only three months away. His opponent this time around is anything but a pushover. So how's your job in Sacramento working out?"

"W-e-l-l...Believe it or not, the State Assembly's got some of the biggest egos I've ever worked for. Even bigger than the ones in D.C."

"Lucky you!" he taunted.

"Thanks a lot!" As she spoke, he imagined the corners of her small mouth curving upward ever so slightly, as they always did when she smiled at something he'd said. He wondered why she'd called out of the blue. And hoped it was because she wanted to re-start their affair.

"I've missed you," he said.

"And I've missed you. We had some good times, didn't we?"

"We did."

Three years before, when she began working in the Congressman's office, he had asked her to lunch. Why? Because she was cute, with bright blue eyes and short, curly blonde hair. Even though they barely knew one another, she began to share her thoughts about a number of very personal subjects as they picked at their salads. One of these was the state of her marriage.

"My husband and I met in high school," she said. "Now we have nothing in common. He cleans swimming pools for a living— and spends most evenings drinking beer and watching baseball games on TV. Meanwhile, I'm in the study, reviewing legislation or streaming movies on my tablet."

"It doesn't sound like much of a relationship," he said.

She met his gaze.

"It isn't."

The next day, he walked into her office and closed the door behind him. There was a sofa next to her desk. He sat there and looked her in the eyes.

"I'm lonely, too," he lied.

Within a few minutes, she was in his arms on the sofa. As they held each other, he couldn't believe how good her wandering tongue felt in his mouth. I want more of this, he told himself. A lot more.

Several times a week, they would slip away to her apartment, which was just down the street from the Congressman's office. After her husband asked why the sheets on their bed always seemed to be rumpled, he began getting a room for them at a nondescript motel on the edge of the desert.

She was smart, with a wonderful sense of humor. If he wasn't happily married, he might have fallen for her. But as things stood, the relationship had more to do with sex than anything else. He thought she felt the same way. But one afternoon as they stood on opposite sides of the motel room's bed, slipping their clothes back on, she asked:

"Where's this going?"

He looked her way but didn't answer.

She circled the bed then and embraced him.

"I'm in love with you," she whispered, staring into his eyes.

He took her face in his hands.

"I feel the same way about you."

As he drove away from the motel, he scowled at himself in the rear view mirror and shook his head. Why did I let this get so complicated? he asked himself.

The next time they rendezvoused at the motel, their sex was as great as ever. As they lay naked next to one another afterwards, she said: "I'm leaving my husband."

She studied his poker face. "What are you going to do?".

He hesitated. "I don't know. This is happening so fast."

"I can't stand the thought of your wife ever touching you again," she said. "It makes me want to scratch the bitch's eyes out."

Oh my God! he thought. What have I gotten myself into? At the same time, though, he relished the fact that she felt so strongly about having him to herself.

When they met again a few days later, he sat on the edge of the bed and began to slip off his shoes.

I've moved into my own place," she said. "We can meet there from now on. And I've booked a weekend cruise next month to Mexico."

"A cruise to Mexico?"

She flashed an impish grin.

"Yes. For you and I."

He grasped her hand.

"That sounds wonderful."

Abruptly, her smile disappeared.

"You need to make a decision about your marriage by the time we sail," she said.

He let go of her hand and got to his feet.

"Priscilla and I have been together for eight years. You need to give me some time to figure this out."

She pushed her lips tightly together. "Until you do," she said, "I think it'd be best if we stopped meeting like this."

Later that week, he paused in the doorway to her office.

"Got a few minutes?"

"Sure."

While he sat on the sofa, she stayed in the chair behind her desk.

"My wife is taking this very hard."

She watched him. "What are you trying to tell me?"

"I'm not going on the cruise."

Seeing that her eyes were filling with tears, he stood and walked back down the hallway to his desk.

After that, they barely spoke unless their work required it. Two months later, she departed the desert for her new job in Sacramento.

*   *   *

"I have some things to tell you," she said over the phone, suddenly sounding very serious. "Do you have a few minutes?"

"Of course."

"I harmed you," she said. "And I've called to make amends. I threw myself at you. It didn't matter that you were married. All I cared about was making you mine. No matter who got hurt. I caused you to be unfaithful to your wife. I used our sex to try and steal you away from her.

"If I hadn't gotten the job in Sacramento and moved away, I would've succeeded. You would be mine."

He wasn't about to tell her that he had never loved her, that it was all a physical attachment as far as he was concerned.

"Why did you call now, over two years after the fact?" he said.

"Because I wanted to make sure both of us have put this behind us. You see, I'm coming back to the desert."

His grip on the cellphone tightened.

"I'm working on Jason Johnson's campaign. You know who he is, I'm sure—the man who's running against the Congressman."

"So you switched parties?"

"Jason's a very persuasive guy. After he wins the election, we're getting married."

"Don't count your chickens before they hatch," he warned.

"Which chickens are you talking about?" she said. "Winning the election chickens or marrying the new Congressman chickens?"

"All the damn chickens!"

At that, they both burst out laughing.

He arose early the next morning after a restless night. The first thing he did was raise the bedroom window's blinds so that he could see the clay pot in the morning light. It was empty. But he knew they would be back.

MORTIFICATION AND MIRACLES

I was still a virgin when I began my junior year in college. But then I met Linda in the Faulkner aisle of the campus library.

"Come over to my place tonight," she said. "We'll eat spaghetti and smoke hash and talk about Light In August." She took a step closer to me in the narrow space between the bookcases, a Mona Lisa smile on her lips. "I promise you'll have the time of your life," she whispered, gazing into my eyes.

Linda was skinny as a scarecrow and had long, stringy brown hair that she didn't seem to wash that often. But she kept her promise--and changed my world.

In no time at all, I'd slept with several other English Lit majors and discovered a place to drink beer all afternoon. Right across the street from the college, in an ugly gray concrete shopping center that had trouble keeping other tenants, was a bar where no one ever bothered to ask for my I.D.

That's where I met Jerry, a bearded Vietnam vet in his mid-twenties. I often ran into him at the bar. We'd drink for a while, then slip down the empty alley behind the building and light up a fat joint.

One afternoon, Jerry was telling me about getting high and using his service revolver to rid his Da Nang hut of the huge water rats that infested it. Suddenly he paused.

"Ever dropped LSD?" he said.

I stared blankly at him.

He tried again: "You ever eaten acid?"

I hadn't. But I was embarrassed to admit it. This was 1969. War protesters were bravely burning their draft cards and marching defiantly through the streets of America's cities. Hundreds of thousands more were planning to visit Upstate New York that summer to take part in the biggest rock festival ever. Meanwhile, I hadn't tried LSD. My youth was slipping through my fingers.

"Of course," I finally answered.

"One of the dudes I live with just got hold of some outtasight Orange Sunshine. Wanna try it?"

"Right now?" My head began to fill with recollections of stories I'd read on the front page of the National Enquirer--stories about acid freaks who stared into the sun until they went blind or jumped off the top of skyscrapers or ripped their own eyeballs out with tablespoons.

He frowned at me. "What's wrong?"

I shook my head. "Nothing."

"Then let's head over to my place."

When we arrived at the apartment, his two housemates were slumped on a sofa in the living room, strangely quiet. The pair, who both had long hair that fell over their shoulders, didn't acknowledge our presence. Instead, they stared straight ahead as if in some kind of trance.

"Come on," Jerry said, disappearing down a hallway.

He stood in his bedroom, displaying two tiny orange capsules in his open palm, when I walked through the doorway.

"Take your pick," he said.

"Jerry--" I began.

He squinted at me. "You sure you've tripped before?"

Without another word, I took one of the capsules from his hand and swallowed it.

Soon the bedroom's walls began to waver like thick strips of white Jello caught in an earthquake.

"Let's get outta here," he said.

Arms outstretched like a blind man trying to find his way, I followed Jerry unsteadily back down the hallway, past the comatose figures on the sofa and out the front door. We got into his Corvair van and he began driving.

As dusk settled over Orange County, chemically-induced pink jackrabbits began appearing everywhere. They ran beside the van, scurried in the headlights' glare, leaped from the freeway's overpasses.

"Wish I had my fuckin' pistol," Jerry said. "It looks like a shooting gallery out there."

It was a weeknight, and the streets of Newport Beach were nearly deserted. As soon as we parked next to the ocean and began walking towards the pier, purple and orange plants started squirming out of the sand. While the colorful cactus-like apparitions wiggled and grew at our feet, the beach around them became overrun with luminescent crabs and lobsters, flopping over each other, claws clicking at us.

Jerry began to laugh hysterically. "Look at those fuckers!" he shouted.

"I'm looking," I said. I wasn't enjoying myself, though; the drug-induced creatures were more than a little unnerving.

On our return to the Chevy, he leaned into the driver's window and pulled a joint from under the dashboard. We passed it back and forth, taking long tokes. Halfway through the number, we started to relax.

"How much longer you think this'll last?" I said.

He shrugged. "I'm havin' a good time. What about you?"

"To tell you the truth--"

I stopped. Jerry was gaping past me.

I glanced over my shoulder. A police car, its headlights off, slowly pulled up next to us. Jerry quickly flicked the smoldering roach onto the darkened sand.

We faced the two cops, who looked us over with the help of their flashlights.

"What are you up to?" one of them said.

"Walkin' on the beach," Jerry replied. "Any law against that?"

"We'll ask the questions."

While his partner stayed back and kept his light on us, the cop moved closer. I felt myself trembling as he stopped in front of me.

"Let me smell your breath," he demanded.

After I breathed on him, he smelled Jerry's breath, too, and then took a step backwards.

"Where's the dope?"

Jerry stared at the cop. "Whatta you talkin' about?"

"You know what the fuck I'm talking about." The cop paused. "A Corvair like yours has been spotted during several burglaries in this neighborhood. That gives us probable cause to search."

"Search away," Jerry said nonchalantly.

Taking him at his word, the cop peered into every corner and crevice of the Chevy. Despite the cold sea air, I felt drops of sweat breaking out on my forehead.

The cop finally gave up on the van.

"I know that joint's around here," he barked, pushing past us. He began shining the flashlight at the very same spot on the sand where Jerry had flipped the damn thing.

Since I was raised a Catholic, I did what came naturally and began to ask God to save us from ourselves—until I caught a glimpse of the patrol car out of the corner of my eye. It was covered with red and maroon snakes. They crawled all over the roof, which was so crowded that a few were dropping to the asphalt.

"Christ!" Jerry whispered under his breath.

While we gazed at the snakes, the cop came up from behind us.

"You're lucky this time," he said as he examined our driver's licenses. "But I don't want to find either one of you in Newport Beach." He shined the blinding light in our eyes. "Ever again."

A few of the reptiles fell to the pavement and scurried into the shadows as the patrol car disappeared across the empty parking lot.

"Let's get the hell out of here," I pleaded.

Jerry reached into his trouser pocket.

"Fuck!" he shouted.

"What's wrong?"

"My key!" He looked angry and confused at the same time. "My key's gone!"

"Is it in the ignition?"

He reached through the open window and felt the side of the steering column.

"Nope. It must've fallen out of my pocket while we were walkin' on the beach."

I looked out over the acres of darkened sand between us and the pier. "We'd better start thumbing," I said.

Jerry shook his head. "Didn't you hear that pig? They'll lock us up if they see you and me again."

We trekked back and forth across the beach for what must have been an hour, until I'd completely given up hope of ever finding the key. In the meantime, I had plenty of time to think a few things over. What was I doing here? Why, abusing my body, the Temple of God. With LSD! Those National Enquirer headlines flashed across my mind. I was so mortified that I felt sick at heart.

At that moment, I looked down. The key was laying at my feet, glistening in the light of the full moon that had just risen.

The van seemed to fly down the freeway as we laughed about all the fun we'd had.

"You know what?" Jerry said as he fiddled with the radio's dial. "I never thought we'd find that key."

I nodded. "It was a miracle."

He glanced at me and grinned wryly.

"So right you are, Peter. The LSD showed you the key. Just like it hid the joint from the cops."

I stared silently out the windshield.

At the time, I had a steady girlfriend, a high school senior who was ditzy enough to believe she'd actually seen Jesus Christ once while smoking a joint. Ever since, she'd refused to use marijuana. But she loved to drink beer. So I'd buy a six-pack of Lucky Lager or Falstaff and we'd spend Saturday night at the drive-in, feeling each other out. She never let me get past third base. But I liked her anyway. She was the first person I'd ever met who depended on me. During her period, when the cramps got bad, she'd call and beg me to come by.

"Please," she'd implore, "you're the only one who understands."

When the movies ended, we'd leave the drive-in and I'd park my '59 Ford station wagon in front of the apartment building where she lived with her parents and younger brother. There was another apartment building under construction across the street. She'd wonder, glassy-eyed with romance, if someday we might live there together.

"You never can tell," I'd answer, slipping my hand into her panties.

Right after graduation, we broke up and she began dating one of her former teachers. It was a whirlwind affair; six months later, they got married. For all I know, they might have moved into that new apartment building.

The day after I took the acid, I was supposed to meet her for lunch at a hamburger stand a block from the high school campus. But I didn't feel like meeting anyone. The acid had drained me, physically and mentally. All I felt like doing was double-bolting the door of my bedroom and sleeping for a week.

When she arrived, though, arms loaded with textbooks, I was waiting. She stopped smiling as soon as she got a good look at me.

"Your eyes are funny," she said.

"I stayed up kind of late last night."

"Were you out drinking?"

"No." I hesitated. "I dropped some acid."

"Acid?" she repeated, as if in a daze. Her books tumbled onto the sidewalk in a heap as she took me in her arms and started to sob.

"Why'd you do it?" she asked.

"Search me."

"Haven't you ever read those stories in the National Enquirer," she said, "about the couples who took LSD and had babies that looked like monsters?" She pressed her tear-stained face to my chest.

As I contemplated the possibility that she and I would someday be the parents of a monster infant, I, too, began to cry.

"I'll never do it again," I promised tearfully. And you know what? I almost prayed that I'd keep that promise.

CARNIVAL!

The crescent-shaped bay's aquamarine waters lap at the edge of a vast desert. Just past the shoreline, two dozen weather-beaten skiffs rest haphazardly on the sand in the late afternoon sunlight. Huddled beyond the boats is a collection of makeshift wood frame buildings. Inside the dwellings, the fishermen lie exhausted in their beds. They had awoken before sunup to row out of the bay through the darkness. Crouching for hours in the shallow bellies of the boats, they prayed that a grouper or dorado would become trapped within the nets. Few of these prayers were answered today; most of the vessels returned with little to show for their crews' efforts.

Despite this inauspicious eve, one of the most anticipated holy day of the year has almost arrived. On the following morning, the villagers will observe the Day of the Fish, a celebration whose origins reach back to the pagan rites of their ancestors.

To mark this holiday, a traveling carnival always visits the village. It's only a collection of transparently fraudulent freaks and a rickety Ferris wheel, purchased third-hand years before in America. For the villagers, though, the carnival is a magical intrusion, a glimpse of the mystery and wonder of the outside world, delivered to their humble community by the half-dozen red and blue trucks which annually appear on the holy day's eve.

While the fishermen sleep, the worn-out trucks rumble past the shacks and stop next to the graveyard and the church. In the fading light, the carnies erect the Ferris wheel and a large tent made of striped canvas. When these chores are finished, they gather around a huge bonfire. With no bars or prostitutes here, the men squat on the bare ground and noisily share bottles of raicilla.

As his companions pass the moonshine, a young man slips into the surrounding shadows. He follows a rutted road past the dark shacks. There is no electricity or indoor plumbing here; the smells of kerosene and human waste fill the air. On this night, he is feeling sorry for himself. He has been away from home for six months, and he doesn't get along with the other carnies. They make fun of the fact that he still has no beard to shave. "Maybe it's a girl in disguise!" they laugh, scratching their crotches and leering at him.

"Idiots!" he mutters as he trudges down the empty street, shaking his head in disgust.

At that moment, his foot slips into a large pothole, sending him tumbling to the hard ground.

"O-o-o-h!" he cries, reaching down to grasp his ankle.

A teenage girl sits across the road, in front of one of the unlighted shacks, watching him. She wonders if he has broken something. Yet she is too shy to stand and come to his aid.

He struggles to his feet. "Shit!" he exclaims as he tries to place some weight on the ankle. He begins to bounce about in the dark on his good leg.

The girl giggles in spite of herself.

He stops. "Who's that?" he asks the night. "Who's cruel enough to take pleasure in my misery?"

"I'm sorry. It's just that you look so funny...hopping around like a jackrabbit."

He bounds towards the sound of her voice.

"Like a jackrabbit, huh?" he repeats indignantly.

"I said I was sorry!" She pauses. "Are you all right?"

"I'll live. How could you see me? There's no moon out tonight."

"I can see in the dark," she says.

"Really?"

"Oh, yes. My mother says it's a gift from God."

Or the devil, he tells himself.

"Can you see my face?"

"Of course."

He leans closer to her. "I wish I could see yours."

She glances back at the shack's door.

"You'd better go," she says, lowering her voice as she turns to him. "If my father catches us here—"

"Are you going to the carnival tomorrow?"

"Yes."

"That's where I'm from. I'll see you there."

For a moment, he continues to stare in her direction, trying to make out her features. Then he gingerly begins to limp down the road in the direction of the graveyard.

After he has gone, she stands and steps through the dilapidated shack's doorway. It has only one room, and she must step over her sleeping parents and brothers as she moves to her pallet in a corner.

Slipping under a single sheet, she rests her head on a rolled-up blanket and stares at the ceiling. She can make out every mismatched board above her head. As she recalls the young man's handsome face, she sighs. She has never had a boyfriend. A tingle of nervous excitement runs up her body. I'll never be able to sleep, she tells herself. She can't wait until the morning comes and the carnival begins.

*   *   *

Dawn breaks over the sea in a burst of blinding sunlight. The glare and heat fill the shack's east-facing windows and penetrate its crooked, crevice-filled walls. Even though her father isn't fishing today, the young woman and her mother rose in the dark as usual and began preparing breakfast. The sun rises while the family takes their places around a plastic table, sitting on assorted chairs and stools. They gobble up tortillas and fried fish and sip coffee from cups with broken handles.

65

Out of the corner of her eye, the girl watches her father. His skin, tanned by his livelihood, seems almost as dark as his black hair. A large moustache droops under his nose and over his upper lip. When he sets his intense stare on her, she quickly lowers her face.

Like her four younger brothers, she resembles her mother, a tiny figure who sits at the opposite end of the cramped table. The woman's Aztec lineage is evident in her round eyes, long nose and high cheekbones. In order to avoid her husband's glare, she directs her gaze nervously around the table from one child to another.

When they finish eating, the family begins to dress for the carnival. The women pull on their brightly colored Sunday skirts while the man and his sons button up their long-sleeved embroidered shirts.

It is already very hot as the man leads his family down the front steps of the shack and onto the dusty road. On top of his head rests a short-brimmed straw hat with a tassel hanging at its rear. When the man spots a neighbor, he nods solemnly, causing the tassel to swing crazily behind his back. It's as if some insect hangs there, fighting to escape.

The girl can already see the carnival in the distance. The canvas tent and Ferris wheel are taller than any other structures in the village; taller, even, than the bell tower of the church. She once again feels a tingle of excitement.

When the Mass is finished, the villagers file out of the sanctuary and form a semi-circle in front of the tent. The priest stands alone in their midst. On a small, low wooden table before him sets a metal basin filled with seawater.

As the girl and the rest of her family join their neighbors, she covers her mouth with her hand. The young man is standing behind the priest with the rest of the carnies. He turns his head this way and that, studying each face in the crowd. She blushes as his gaze passes over her. But then she remembers that he can't possibly recognize her; it was dark as a cave last night.

"In the name of the Father, and the Son, and the Holy Ghost," the priest intones, blessing the basin's contents with his upraised right hand, "we celebrate the sea's bounty and thank our Savior for his mercy."

The girl and the rest of the villagers make the Sign of the Cross. The priest lifts the basin in his slim arms. Stepping among the families, he dips his hand into the holy seawater and shakes it from his fingers onto the congregants. She feels the coolness of the water dripping down her forehead and crosses herself again.

Once the priest passes them, the villagers step away. Relatives and friends call to one another while the barkers inside the tent shout their spiels.

"Over here, folks, over here!" insists a short, fat man with a red bandana wrapped about his large head. "Inside"—he points at a flap of black canvas behind him—"is the strangest sight your eyes will ever behold. It's a baby that's half man and half fish. Seeing is believing!"

Near the Ferris wheel, which is already surrounded by those waiting for their turn to ride, two old men appear. One holds an accordion in his hands, the other cradles a battered guitar. The pair nod their wide-brimmed straw hats at one another. Then they start to play. Shouts of exhilaration greet the simple, rousing sound of the music as it drifts across the lot.

The girl stands next to her brothers while her father passes out pesos to each of them. He glares at her as he drops the coins in her open palm.

"I don't want to see you talking to any men," he warns her sternly. "You're only fourteen years old."

She watches him silently.

"Did you hear me?" he barks.

She nods quickly and disappears into the crowd. As she walks away, she whispers under her breath.

"'Only fourteen years old?'" she repeats disdainfully. "I guess he's forgotten that Mother was fourteen years old when I was born."

She stops in her tracks. The young man is standing only a few feet in front of her. A cardboard tray full of churros hangs from his neck by a length of rope. He is handing one of the sweets to a little girl. After he takes her money, he adjusts the rope with a scowl and begins to walk away.

She hesitates, watching his back.

"Here! Churros man!"

When he turns towards her voice, she is standing in front of him, offering a coin.

He hands her one of the sweets, wrapped in a piece of newspaper. As he takes the coin, he brushes his fingertips along the inside of her palm.

"Your voice sounds familiar," he says. "Haven't we talked before?"

"Maybe."

"You're the girl who can see in the dark."

"Now that I can see you," he continues, "I know your gift comes from God. The devil couldn't have anything to do with someone so beautiful."

She stares at him, transfixed. This all seems like a wonderful dream.

"Yes, like one of the angels." The young man takes her hand and squeezes it.

She pulls it away as she glances behind her. "My father—" she begins.

"I can get off work for a little while. Will you come and meet me?"

"Where?"

He nods at the red and blue trucks which are parked side-by-side at the end of the lot.

She stares into his large dark eyes and bites her lower lip.

"I'll see you in a half hour," he says.

In a daze, the girl wanders through the carnival. Finding herself at the Ferris wheel, she hands her last coin to the carnie. She is oblivious to the cries of the other riders as they rock back and forth above the village. The thrill in her heart is much more frightening than any feeling which this contraption could produce. She is so distracted that she forgets the churro in the gondola when she steps out.

Walking alone as the crowd thins out, she passes the church and the graveyard. Finally she reaches the far end of the clearing where the trucks are parked. Moving in the shadows between them, she feels as though she is lost in a maze. She remembers a tale she once heard of a labyrinth her ancestors had constructed in one of their great cities. When the Spaniards arrived, they herded the captured and now unarmed Aztec warriors into the maze, where they were hunted down like animals and murdered.

Why would I remember that story now? she tells herself. The thought unsettles her.

"Hello."

Startled, she turns. The young man is standing behind her, a wide grin filling his thin face.

"You surprised me."

"Just like you surprised me last night."

He takes her hand and leads her into the sunlight. The trucks separate them from the carnival. Beyond the village, the desert stretches towards a distant range of boulder-strewn hills.

He has spread a quilt on the sand. He kneels on it. Reluctantly, she sits beside him.

"What's your name?" he says.

"Xochitl."

"I'm Julio."

As he watches her, she glances away towards the hills.

"You've never been with a man before, have you?"

Swallowing nervously, she turns her eyes back to him.

He puts his arm around her shoulder and pulls her to him. Cupping her face in his free hand, he kisses her on the lips. He feels her arms across his back.

"You're so beautiful," he whispers.

He unbuckles his belt and pulls down his trousers. She doesn't resist as he raises her skirt above her waist. Their sex is clumsy, quick and without tenderness.

Her father has followed her here. While Julio penetrates her, he crouches behind one of the trucks, glaring at the pair. He is so filled with rage that he can barely see. He raises his face to the sky.

"God, why did you give me a daughter?" he hisses, between clinched teeth.

When Julio has finished, he gets to his feet and hitches up his trousers. Xochitl pulls her beautiful skirt over her chubby legs. The sounds of the carnival—barkers shouting, musicians strumming their instruments and singing, villagers laughing—drift between the trucks.

"I've got to get back to work," he tells her curtly. "They're going to be looking for me."

She stares at him.

"Julio..." she begins.

"I'll see you later," he says nonchalantly over his shoulder. "I'll find you before we leave."

For several minutes, Xochitl remains seated on the quilt, as still as a statue. Trying to understand what has happened to her. She senses that, somehow, the last few minutes will change her life.

Finally she stands. Instead of returning to the carnival, she crosses the road and enters the empty church. The carnival's sounds follow her through the open doorway. Moving to the first row of pews, she kneels and produces a rosary from a pocket of the skirt. Pinching the beads between her thumb and forefinger, she begins to mechanically recite the formalized prayers which the priest has taught her.

*   *   *

It is past sunset before Xochitl returns to her family's shack. After leaving the church, she spent the afternoon wandering along the shoreline. Her life had seemed so simple before. There was her family and the sea and the desert. There were the neighbors who she had known her whole life, and there was Mass on Sunday. But her life had grown infinitely more complicated, all in one afternoon. She'd been forced to think about right and wrong, about guilt, about love and about herself. Nothing seemed to make sense anymore. It was as if her sex with Julio had left her in the state of an unborn child, uncomprehending and helpless.

While she walked along the bay, she saw the caravan of carnival trucks in the distance, driving away from the village. As she watched, their headlights switched on in the twilight.

"Goodbye, my love," she said aloud. A wind began to rise from the desert.

She pauses now on the steps that lead to the shack's open doorway. Her father will be angry because she was gone so long. Perhaps he will beat her; he has beaten her many times before.

It is black inside the shack, but she can see. Her father crouches next to the doorway, waiting for her return. Sweating profusely, a strange look fills his eyes. Xochitl's body shakes as she stares at him. He is gripping a large metal wrench with both hands.

She turns and steps back down to the road. Her eyes are filling with tears. Why would he want to hurt me? she asks herself. She begins to run. Xochitl passes the darkened church and the graveyard. The sandy lot, empty now, is covered with trash.

She stops running. Ahead, the road disappears into the desert. She knows it continues for many kilometers. There is a town down the road, with stores and restaurants and a hotel. Railroad tracks pass through the town, and trains stop at its station. She has heard that the trains go all the way to the border with the United States.

She turns back to the village. The tears run down her cheeks. She knows she will never see this place again. Xochitl turns her back on the village and begins to follow the road.

THE LITTLE COFFIN

It was late afternoon when I walked into the thrift store on the little desert town's main street and asked the plump, middle-aged lady at the counter if she had any music CDs. I'm a long-haul trucker, and always looking for ways to deep-six the loneliness on the run between California and Walmart's headquarters in northwest Arkansas.

She led me down a cramped aisle past a half-empty glass jewelry counter to a beat-up bookcase filled with plastic DVD cases. In the middle of the movies was a black nylon binder.

After she left, I pulled the binder off the shelf and unzipped it. Inside was page after page of transparent plastic sleeves. Each held a CD.

I walked back to the front of the store.

"Where'd all those CDs come from?" I said.

"If someone falls behind on the rent at one of those big storage facilities, the owners auction off the unit's contents. That's how we got 'em. And lots of other stuff that's here in the store."

Just outside the town was one of the largest Marine bases in the world. The desolation and summer heat must've made it a perfect place for training young soldiers to fight in the Middle East. I'd noticed several storage facilities on the road between the town and the base. Places called Devil Dog Storage and Storage For You, Warrior.

"When a Marine's killed in Afghanistan, is his stuff auctioned off?"

A funny look crossed her face. I guessed my question took her by surprise.

"I suppose so," she said.

"So those CDs you have for sale might've belonged to a dead Marine."

She narrowed her close-set eyes.

"Could be."

"How much you charge for the CDs?"

"Twenty-five cents each. But I'll sell you the binder an' everything in it for five bucks."

I went back to the bookcase. With a shudder, I thought about how much the binder with the CDs resembled a little coffin. I picked it up, paid the lady and went back to my cabin.

The binder's owner had mixed-up tastes: There were CDs by Cecilia Bartoli, Slayer, Judy Collins, Motorhead, Rosanne Cash, Deep Purple, Dolly Parton, The Clash--and lots more besides. Who likes Celine Dion AND Ozzy Osbourne? Johnny Rotten AND Beverly Sills?

Under the light hanging over the kitchen table, I began pulling discs from their sleeves. Those by the "nice" folks were in nice condition. They looked like they'd never been touched. But the punk and heavy metal discs were scuffed and scratched; the surface of some were so scarred that I figured they probably wouldn't play without skipping.

The next morning, I picked up the binder and took the rest of the CDs out of their sleeves. Half the discs were by lady artists with beautiful voices, and half by bands and singers who could get you in the mood to go to war.

I turned back to the binder--and saw for the first time that there was a pocket with something other than a CD tucked inside of it. The edge of a slip of notebook paper was sticking out.

It was covered with lines of rough scrawl. Like entries in a shipping log, the writing consisted of dates and brief notes.

"January 15," read the first entry. "Sandy Denny. Like An Old Fashioned Waltz".

This was one of the discs that lay before me.

For two months, someone had added entries. All of them listed the names of lady singers and the title of their album from the binder.

The last entry, on March 17, said: "Iris Dement. My Life".

Besides the log and the CDs, there was nothing else in the binder. Nothing to tell me who the discs belonged to, why the list of singers and albums had been written down. Or why the rest of the CDs, the punk and rock albums, weren't on the list.

Two weeks later, I stopped in at the thrift store again to take a look around. The lady at the counter pushed her thick lips together when she saw me.

"You know that folder full a' CDs I sold you?" she said. "The Marine's widow's in town, trying to track down the stuff from his storage unit. An' she really wants those CDs."

When I dialed the number the thrift store lady gave me, a woman answered the phone. I told her about buying the binder, and that I'd heard she'd like to have the CDs.

"I really would," she answered. "They mean a lot to me."

Palm trees clustered about an oasis on the edge of town. Beneath the fronds stood a 1950's-era motel and a little adobe building with a restaurant that had a horseshoe-shaped bar.

She sat at the bar. In her mid-thirties—older than I expected—and slim, with long strawberry blonde hair tied into a ponytail that hung halfway down her back.

"I'm sorry about your husband," I said.

She stared at me with her deep blue eyes.

"We'd only been married a month when he shipped out," she said. "We never got a chance to know one another."

She and I ordered cocktails from the bored looking bartender.

"How did you meet?" I asked after the drinks arrived.

"I'm a nurse at the Navy hospital in San Diego. He was badly injured during a training exercise at Camp Pendelton. It's the only time I've ever gotten emotionally involved with a patient." She kept her gaze on me. "He was only twenty-one. I care about all my patients. But with him, it became more than that—and right away. He was a real charmer."

I noticed a tattoo on her left wrist. The name JAMEY had been carved into her flesh.

"Tell me about the CDs."

She shifted on the stool. "After he was discharged from the hospital, we decided to get married. He already had the binder, with his CDs in it—all the loud and nasty stuff. 'Let me give you some of my favorite music to take with you to the Middle East,' I told him. 'It'll help you to get to know me better, even though we'll be thousands of miles apart.'"

I pulled the handwritten list from my shirt pocket and handed it to her.

"This was with the CDs," I said.

She studied it for several minutes, looking at one side and then flipping the page over to see the rest of the writing.

"He must have done this so he could prove to me that he listened to my CDs. How do you like that handwriting?" she said, looking up. "He told me he barely graduated from high school. Here's the proof!"

Then she snapped her fingers at the bartender.

"Another round," she told him.

Halfway through the second bourbon and soda, I asked: "Think the CDs helped him get to know you better?"

She stared at me.

"He already knew me well enough to keep me happy. And that's all anyone can ask for." Her eyes were all that I could see. They seemed to fill the room.

"I'll get the CDs," I said. "They're in my car."

"I'm staying here at the motel," she answered. "Would you mind taking them to my room? I'll get two more drinks and meet you there."

As I walked across the gravel parking lot, the binder in my hand, I tried to sort through what was going on. Maybe she's just lonely, I said to myself.

The door to her room was open. When I entered, she grabbed the binder, took one of the CDs out of its sleeve and slipped it into a portable player on the dresser.

I expected to hear something soft and melodic. But what blasted out of the speakers was the voice of Axl Rose, squealing "WELCOME TO THE JUNGLE!"

"This is one of my favorites," she shouted over the racket, handing me the fresh drink. "I haven't heard it in a long time. Ever since Jamey went overseas."

I clinked my glass against hers.

"To Jamey," I said.

For the first time, she smiled at me.

While the CD kept playing, she suddenly disappeared into the bedroom and closed the door behind her. A few minutes passed. As the next song began, I went to the door and pulled it open.

She was standing in the far corner of the room, next to the bed, her face in her hands.

I stepped forward and put my hand on her shoulder. She turned her eyes, now filled with tears, to me.

"I...I thought that hear...hearing his music again would make me feel better," she stuttered. "But I feel worse than ever."

The Guns N' Roses CD was still blaring in the adjacent room.

"He was so young," she said over the sound of the music. "Too young to die."

"Let's go outside," I said.

I took her hand in mine and led her past the other guest rooms to the edge of the oasis. We stood together in the quiet of the desert twilight. Before us, the western sky was filled with streaks of red.

She turned from the sunset. Once again, I lost myself in the deep blue of her gaze.

We decided to get together later in the week. The thrift store had collected everything they'd purchased from Jamey's storage unit. I loaded the boxes into the trunk of her sedan. She planned to return to San Diego the following day.

That night, we had dinner at the horseshoe-shaped bar and, afterwards, I walked her to her room.

"Let's stay in touch," she said. "I only live three hours away from here."

I nodded. "Let's do that."

Then we wrapped our arms around one another. I looked over her shoulder and through the doorway. The little coffin was setting all by itself on the sofa.

THE MOANING CAVE

Fred smiled stupidly at his own image in the Toyota's rearview mirror. Thank God that restaurant where we stopped for lunch had a well-stocked bar, he told himself. It was amazing how a couple of drinks could improve a person's disposition. For the first time that day, he felt like he was on vacation.

"We're almost to the hotel, aren't we?"

"It's another hundred miles, at least," Jane said.

"Is that all?" The grin remained on his face.

The freeway soon ended; they were now traveling on a narrow two lane road that wound between rolling hillocks Everywhere they looked, there were vineyards and apple orchards.

A large wooden sign came into sight around a bend that spelled out FAMOUS MOANING CAVE. 3 MILES AHEAD.

"That sounds like fun," he said.

She didn't answer.

In a few minutes, the car climbed a steep hill. At the top of the rise stood a long, narrow wooden building.

"Come on," he urged as he climbed out of the Toyota.

"I'm not going," she answered shortly. "I'd rather stay here and take a nap."

He shrugged. "Suit yourself."

The walls inside the building were lined with glass counters displaying various snacks and souvenirs. Just past a self-serve soft drink dispenser was a closed door with the words "Entrance-- Moaning Cave" painted on its surface.

"Can I help you?"

He flinched and looked towards the sound. A young woman stood behind one of the counters, staring at him. He could've sworn she wasn't there when he entered the place.

"Christ, you scared me--" he began.

"Can I help you?" she repeated. Very thin and plain looking, she had the palest skin he'd ever seen.

"I came to see the cave."

"Ten dollars." She held out an open palm and watched him with her strange, colorless eyes.

After he'd handed her the money, she led him to the doorway, produced a key from a pocket in her gray dress and unlocked the door. They followed a narrow passage carved out of solid rock. A row of bare bulbs, mounted overhead, illuminated the space. It was so cramped in several places that he had to turn his body in order to squeeze through.

Abruptly, the passage ended and a stairway began, zig-zagging back and forth as they continued downward. The woman had obviously made this journey many times; she moved briskly from step to step without pausing. Her rapid pace was wearing him out.

"Let's take a break, okay?" he said, breathing heavily.

She glanced over her shoulder.

"Just a little farther," she said, sounding as if she was coaxing along a child.

The stairs ended at a metal platform surrounded by a guardrail. Beyond it, everything was black.

"I'm going to shut off the lights." The guide reached for a switch in the wall. Suddenly they were in total darkness.

"We are at the edge of the abyss," she said.

He heard another click. Several spotlights flashed on overhead, revealing a breathtaking panorama of multi-colored stalactites suspended from the cavern's ceiling and walls.

"What causes the moaning?" he said.

She kept her eyes on him. "The cave moans when someone passes through it who has lost their way."

He smirked. "Are you serious?"

"I think you understand." The sound of her voice echoed through the chamber. Without another word, she started back up the stairway.

In no time at all, she'd disappeared among the shadows. When he finally pushed open the doorway and stepped back into the building, she was still nowhere to be seen.

"What was it like?" Jane said when he returned to the Toyota. He shook his head.

"The guide has a few screws loose. She's been hanging around the inside of that cave way too long! Let's get the hell out of here."

While the car crossed the empty parking lot and disappeared down the hill, he thought he heard a strange noise behind them; a low, rumbling sound. There was something sad about it. Yet the sound lacked any quality that could be called human. Steadily, its volume increased.

As it grew louder, he turned to Jane.

"Do you hear that?"

She glanced up from her smartphone. "What are you talking about?"

He stared into the rearview mirror. There was nothing to see except the tight-lipped glare of his own face. He looked ahead and pressed his foot down hard on the car's gas pedal. But he couldn't leave the moaning behind him. No matter how fast he went, it still filled his ears.

HAPPY LAND

In June of 1970, right after I'd graduated from high school, my parents fell on hard times. My father suffered a nervous breakdown, meaning it would be a long time before he returned to his job as an eighth grade math teacher. A week later, my mother was demoted to part-time at the phone company where she was an information operator.

That night over dinner, she explained what these hard times meant for me, their only child.

"Sheila, I know we've always promised to pay for your college education," Mom told me while Dad sat silently at the end of the table. "Now we can't afford to help. You need to get a job."

As it happened, we lived only a few miles from the most famous amusement park in the world. I spotted an ad in the local newspaper the very next day, announcing that it was hiring. "Join our cast of characters here at Happy Land!" the ad proclaimed.

When I arrived that afternoon at Happy Land's employment office, the middle-aged woman behind the counter looked me up and down. I was barely five feet tall and, in those days, more than a little chubby.

"Here at Happy Land, our employees play a cast of characters," she explained. "Unfortunately, you're not a fit for any of the characters we're hiring right now."

"Are you sure?"

She glanced down at a clipboard on the counter top. "There is one position that might fit you," she said. "We need a maid at the hotel."

Ever since I was a little girl, I'd helped Mom keep our apartment clean. And I was good at it. "That sounds fine," I said.

"You can start tomorrow." She handed me several forms. "Just fill out this paperwork. And before you leave, stop by the hotel and ask for Irma. She'll get you a uniform."

Irma was a Latina about my mother's age who stared silently at me for a moment once she'd handed over the uniform.

"Girl, have you cleaned before," she demanded forcefully in a thick accent.

I nodded.

She tilted her head to one side as she continued to watch me. "You sure?"

"I'm sure," I replied impatiently.

When I returned to the Happy Land Hotel the next morning, Irma gave me my keys, showed me my locker and where the linens and towels were stored and took me to the cart I'd be using. Pushing it ahead of me, I followed her into a nearby service elevator that stopped at the fourth floor.

She pointed down the empty hallway. "Girl, you see those rooms? Those are your rooms. When you get done, you come and see me."

I'd never before been inside of a hotel room--much less one in a high-end place like this. When I entered the first room I was to clean, I stopped in my tracks. Before me was a picture window that provided a sweeping view of the expansive swimming pool below. I wandered about, admiring the beautiful furniture, plush carpeting and handsome bathroom fixtures. What a nice place to work! I thought.

In a few hours, I found Irma in the laundry room.

"I'm done with my rooms."

"What?" she replied loudly, startling me. "Girl, let me tell you something."

"My name's Sheila," I interrupted.

"Girl," she continued, "you're working too fast. If you clean six rooms, they'll give you seven. If you clean seven rooms, they'll give you eight. Besides that, you'll make the other girls look bad. Because of you, everyone will have to clean more rooms!"

She paused for a moment, studying me.

"If you can keep your mouth shut, you can earn some extra money. Want to make some extra money?"

I returned her gaze, a puzzled look on my face.

"Can you keep your mouth shut?" she demanded to know.

"Yes!" I replied nervously.

It wasn't long before a bell hop, dressed in one of those outfits from an old Philip Morris ad with a bow tie, rows of buttons on his chest and a funny little hat, strode towards me as I pushed the cart to my next room. He was past forty and no taller than me.

"I heard you can clean a room fast," he said. "Show me a clean room."

After he inspected the room, he glanced down at his wristwatch.

"Come back in an hour and clean the room again," he said.

"But it's already clean," I protested.

"Trust me," he said with a smirk. "It'll need to be cleaned again."

A few minutes later, a man in a business suit stepped out of the elevator with a tall, elegant-looking blonde woman on his arm. They went to the room I'd shown the bell hop and disappeared inside.

What's going on? I asked myself.

An hour later, I stopped at the door of the room, knocked and announced loudly: "Housekeeping". When no one responded, I used my pass key to enter.

The room was empty. The sheets and blankets had been pulled off the bed and tossed on the floor. Moving closer, I saw that the mattress cover was spotted with stains.

As I finished making the bed for the second time that day, the bell hop appeared in the open doorway.

"I told you it'd need to be cleaned," he said with a wink. He stepped forward and placed a five dollar bill next to me on the fresh sheet.

"Come back in an hour and clean it again," he said.

*　　*　　*

I didn't think much about the immorality of the shenanigans that were going on until a week later. I entered a room right after the hooker and her john had left. Setting in plain sight on a nightstand next to the unmade bed and its dirty sheets was a brown leather wallet. I picked it up, intending to turn it in at lost and found. But first I rifled through its contents. My curiosity had gotten the best of me. Perhaps there was something in the wallet that would give me a clue as to what kind of man paid for sex with a stranger.

According to the drivers license, his name was Gaylen Eddy, born on October 15, 1930. He was quite handsome--a dead ringer for Tab Hunter, the Hollywood actor. "North American Director of Sales, National Heavy Forge, Oakland CA" stated his business card. This meant nothing to me. What's a forge? I thought. There were business cards for other men, too, as well as several credit cards.

The next thing I found made me wish I hadn't looked in the wallet. It was a family portrait, obviously snapped by a professional photographer. Smiling at the camera was Eddy. At his side sat a strikingly beautiful young woman with long, curly red hair and, between them, a darling little towheaded boy, perhaps five years old.

Why would someone with all of this sneak off to meet a prostitute? I couldn't get my head around it.

The next time I saw the bell hop, I asked him: "Where do these men come from?"

"Some are in town for a business convention. And some are on vacation with their wives and kids. While their families spend the day next door in Happy Land, they're getting happy, too."

Seeing the shock in my eyes, he stopped grinning.

"How old are you?"

"Eighteen."

"Let me tell you something, young lady," he said. "This is just the beginning. For as long as you live, human nature will disappoint you."

No longer playing the role of the smart ass bell hop, he stared at me a moment longer before he turned and walked towards the elevator.

*   *   *

When I was in the sixth grade, I began keeping a diary. Ever since, I'd faithfully recorded the ups and downs of my young life. After I started the job at the hotel, I literally turned a page and launched the diary's newest chapter. "I'm making my own money," I wrote. "Some of it's 'dirty', but it's mine. Soon, I'll be going to college. So, I'm feeling pretty good about myself. But there's something I still need to do--LOSE WEIGHT!"

Almost overnight, I ended most of my bad habits. No more candy or snacks between meals. Cottage cheese instead of fully loaded baked potatoes. Oatmeal instead of pancakes and syrup. Working as a maid forced me to end one of my worst habits-- avoiding physical activity. I was now using muscles I didn't even know I had in order to get the rooms cleaned. I also took advantage of my breaks and lunch to stride briskly in my maid uniform on the sidewalks that surrounded Happy Land and the hotel.

One afternoon as I passed the amusement park's entrance, I heard a voice behind me.

"Hey, slow down!"

I turned to face a young man in his early twenties with long black hair, a thick beard and deep blue eyes.

"You're a fast one," he said.

"I don't have much time. I'm on my break."

"Mind if I join you?"

"If you can keep up."

As we walked side-by-side, he told me his name was Ruben.

"How long you been working at the hotel?"

"Since the beginning of the summer."

"You walk every day?"

I nodded as we slipped past a group of children wearing Happy Land caps.

"I'm always around here," he said. "It's funny I never bumped into you before. Want to grab lunch some time?"

"Sounds like fun. But I'm on a diet. I bring my own food to work."

"The hotel's coffee shop has some nice salads." He paused. "I think we should get to know each other."

There was something I hoped to accomplish during the summer that I hadn't dared write down in my diary: lose my virginity. I'd had very few boyfriends. But I figured that would change once I lost some weight. Now I'd met someone, even though I was still on the heavy side.

*   *   *

He was waiting in one of the coffee shop's snug booths, surrounded by tourists who were taking a break from their visit to Happy Land, when I arrived the next day.

"Do you work around here?" I asked after I'd slipped in next to him.

He hesitated, as though the question had taken him by surprise.

"Well..." His voice trailed off for a moment as he scratched at his beard. "Sort of."

"Why were you hanging around the entrance to Happy Land?"

He leaned close to me, until his face was just a few inches from mine.

"I was spying on the place," he whispered.

The feel of his breath, gently caressing my cheek, made me tingle all over.

"Spying?"

He looked over his shoulder to make sure the family from Omaha in the adjacent booth wasn't listening in.

"Ever heard of the Peace and Love Party?" he said.

I shook my head.

"We're a revolutionary organization of young people fed up with what's going on."

At that moment, a waitress appeared and we each ordered an iced tea.

"'What's going on?'" I repeated after she left.

"That's right. Haven't you had it with The Establishment and all the things they're doing to ruin the world?" I hadn't kept up with current events. I'd been too busy cleaning rooms and trying to lose weight.

"What exactly are you talking about?" I said.

He suddenly seemed angry. "I'm talking about the war in Vietnam," he snapped. "You know what our soldiers are doing over there? Murdering innocent people and turning the local women into whores. I'm talking about the pig businessmen who are ripping off The People every second of every day. I'm talking about the racism and poverty that's everywhere."

He made a slashing motion with his hand, as if he was lopping off the heads of the soldiers and the pig businessmen.

"It all has to change," he said in an ominous tone.

I thought of Gaylen Eddy. He certainly was a pig. Maybe Ruben and his friends were on to something.

"What does all that have to do with spying on Happy Land?" I said.

"Most people don't seem to know or care about the bullshit that's going down. We're going to wake them up--do something so dramatic that they won't be able to ignore our message of Peace and Love.

"August 6 is the twenty-fifth anniversary of the day the pigs dropped an atomic bomb on the people of Hiroshima during World War II," he continued. "That afternoon, we're going to invade Happy Land--and take over the hotel."

"Oh my God!" I covered my mouth with the palm of my hand. "That's next week!"

"Don't worry," he said. "We're not going to hurt anyone. We just want to get on the TV news."

"What are you going to do at the hotel?"

"Tell the employees to go home. Thanks to us, you'll have the afternoon of August 6 off." He leered at me. "For once in their miserable lives, the pig guests will have to fend for themselves."

He reached out and took my hand. "Think you could help me?" he asked, studying my face.

"What do you want me to do?"

"Find out if the pigs suspect anything. That's all."

"Sure," I said.

"We're having a planning meeting tonight at my place. Can you come?"

I stared at his handsome face and nodded.

*   *   *

That afternoon after work, he met me in the hotel's parking lot. I steered my '58 Ford Fairlane onto the avenue and followed his VW bug to his apartment. The place was filled with other young people. They were passing around jug bottles of wine and talking excitedly about the upcoming takeover of Happy Land--and the good news they'd just heard. The park's management had eliminated its dress code for visitors. That meant the invaders wouldn't have to get haircuts or shave in order to infiltrate the place.

While the rest of the conspirators went over the logistics for August 6, Ruben took my hand, led me to his bedroom and closed the door behind us. It was a mess. Discarded articles of clothing littered the floor and the little bed was unmade. My instincts told me to start cleaning, but I realized this wasn't the time for that.

He pulled open a drawer in a nightstand next to the bed and produced a fat joint. While I watched, he lit it and then handed it to me. I'd never gotten high before. I sucked in a mouth full of fumes--and began to cough uncontrollably.

He took the joint from my fingers. "Come over here," he said, putting his arm around my shoulder and guiding me to the edge of the bed. We sat next to one another on the mattress.

"Short tokes," he said softly, handing the reefer to me again.

I did much better this time. When we finished it, he dropped the roach in an ash tray and began to massage the back of my neck. "Does that feel good?" he whispered into my ear.

Without answering, I turned to him, placed my hand on the side of his face and kissed him on the lips. We silently slipped out of our clothes and got into the narrow bed. He was the perfect lover, tender and experienced.

Afterwards, he cradled me in his arms.

"I think I love you," he said.

I stared into his eyes. "I think I love you, too."

*　　　*　　　*

Every day after work, I'd drive to his apartment and we would get high and make love. At some point during each of my visits, he'd ask if the pigs suspected that a takeover of the hotel was eminent. "I don't think so," I'd tell him. Of course, the only people I had any interaction with were Irma, the bell hop and guests asking for an extra towel. I had my doubts about how valuable my information could be.

When I arrived at his place on the afternoon of August 5, Ruben seemed uncharacteristically nervous.

"Heard anything?" he asked anxiously.

I shook my head, but that didn't satisfy him.

"You sure?"

I nodded. "I haven't heard a thing."

He led me into his bedroom. But this time, he didn't bring out a joint and there was very little foreplay. As he penetrated me, I could tell that his heart wasn't in it. Once we were through, he abruptly stood and pulled on his jeans.

"You'd better go," he said. "I've got lots to do tonight."

He has so much on his mind, I told myself as I drove home. After the invasion's over, he'll go back to being the man I love.

*   *   *

Nothing seemed out of the ordinary the next morning at the hotel. But just before noon, Irma found me cleaning the toilet in one of my rooms and told me to go to the first floor. When I arrived, most of the other maids were already there. Before us stood an older man in a business suit and, next to him, a police officer.

"I'm Gene Stubble, the general manager of this hotel," the man announced. "The reason I've called you here is to let you know we're going to be evacuating our guests."

The other maids glanced, wide-eyed, at one another.

"We'd like you all to go home," he continued, "and come back tomorrow morning."

"What's going on?" someone asked.

"I can't tell you any more," Stubble said. "Now please leave the property immediately."

In the lobby, the guests were being led outside to waiting buses. I rushed to my car. I had to warn Ruben that, somehow, the police knew about the Peace and Love Party's scheme.

I parked behind the apartment building, climbed up the stairs to his unit on the second floor and banged loudly on the door. When no one answered, I tried to turn the knob, but it was locked.

The only thing I could think to do was return to the hotel. As I approached Happy Land, the traffic slowed to a crawl. Up ahead, crowds of tourists streamed out of the amusement park. The police were directing the cars down a side street that took us in the opposite direction from Happy Land.

When I got home, my parents were sitting on the sofa before the TV. The screen was filled with images of the fleeing crowds, rushing out through the park's gates.

Mom and Dad stood and embraced me. "We were so worried about you," she said breathlessly. "Isn't this horrible?"

All I cared about was finding out if my boyfriend was okay.

The next morning, the hotel looked the same as ever. "It was a big fuss over nothing!" Irma said indignantly. "Just a couple of dozen kids raising hell. All they did was hang a Viet Cong flag on the roof of the carousel and run away."

"Did they get inside the hotel?"

"No! Like I said, Girl, they ran away."

At lunch time, I drove to Ruben's apartment. Once again, there was no answer to my knocks. For the next three days, I stopped by. On the fourth day, an old woman saw me at his door.

"He's gone," she told me.

"Gone?"

"Yeah. He moved out the night before those crazy kids tried to take over Happy Land."

A few days later, the bell hop stopped before me as I dropped an armful of dirty sheets into my cart.

"What's wrong?" he asked.

"I don't know what you're talking about," I replied impatiently.

"You look so sad. Like you've lost your best friend."

He pulled on the sleeve of his tunic until he could see his wristwatch.

"A convention of insurance agents rolled into town yesterday," he said, looking up at me. "In fact, one of these fine gentlemen will be here in ten minutes.

"Got a clean room?"

THE LOST MEN

The demon comes every night. He is white and his eyes glow in the dark. And he comes every night, after Mother and Father fall asleep. Jim never sees the demon, even when he's still awake. I ask him.

"Do you see it?" I ask.

"What?" he says.

"The demon, over in that corner. At the end of the bed."

He hasn't seen it, but he screams. Father drags Jim out of bed and hits him on the backs of his legs with the wooden coathanger. Jim tells him I've been trying to scare him, and Father jerks me up and slaps the backs of my legs. He stops after a little while, if he doesn't smell funny. Once when he smelled funny, he didn't stop until Mother held onto his arm and made him stop.

The demon didn't come until Jim was born. Father didn't hit me, either. He was happy. Mother was happy, too. After I fed the pigs and chickens, I'd help her shell the peas. She'd keep standing and going to the window and saying "Your Father should be here soon."

Father never smelled when he came back from the fields. He'd pick me up when he got home, and the soil rubbed onto my clothes. Mother didn't care. "Guess I'm going to have to do the wash again tomorrow," she'd say. Father smiled. "That's what you get for marrying a poor dirt farmer." Then they'd smile at each other and kiss.

The demon has been in the bedroom since Jim was born. Even back in Oklahoma. He never speaks. He stands at the end of the bed and stares with his glowing eyes until Mother stands over me in the morning. Then the demon climbs into the closet and waits.

The demon wasn't there before Jim came. I'm hoping the new baby that's on the way will make the demon go away, the same as Jim made it come. That's what I hope, but I don't pray for it. Mother says it's selfish to pray for little things.

"When your father hits me, I'm tempted to ask the Lord for strength," she says. "But it's only a little thing. I prayed when the wind came, but I'm sorry I did it now. It was just a test, like moving to California and the new baby are tests. Life's only a test by the Lord, to choose the ones who are worthy."

So I don't pray for the demon to leave. Once, after we got to California, Father drove us to the ocean. I wanted to run into the waves, so the demon would have to let go of me and drown. I asked if I could go into the water. Mother said: "We don't have clothes to spare for swimming. That's for movie stars and the President. Not for folks like us."

Father grabbed her arm and turned her to him. "We're as good as anyone else," he said. "The way you go on, you'd be better off dead." She pulled away from him and held onto my shoulders so tight that I almost cried. Later, she said Father was right.

"I would be better off dead," she told me. "It's only for you and Jim that I've got to live." She began crying, and I clung to her waist and cried.

She cried after the wind killed the horse. We had a brown horse with white spots on its back. It was a gift from Grandfather. We'd ride the horse together, out to Father plowing in the fields. He'd see us, and whistle, and the horse would run right to him. We brought his dinner with us. The sun was always high and hot, and the dirt felt smooth and fine if you touched it.

Once, Father took me out to the fields on a Sunday, after church, and bent over the ground and picked some of it up and let it fall into his other hand.

"It's old soil," he said. "It's worked as hard as men could expect. I only hope it's not completely worn out when it's your time to make a living on this land."

"Why's it getting worn out?" I said.

"The men before me overworked it." He looked strong, squatting in his white shirt and Sunday trousers. "They asked it to do too much. They had no respect for it." He stood and wiped his hands together. "They practically ruined the soil for good and then they sold it to folks like us and moved on to new soil."

"Where'd they go?"

"West," he said. "They're lost men, Joe. They ruin all they touch. In another fifty years, they'll wear out California. Then they'll learn to be fishermen. And they'll be good at that, too. If there's enough of them by then, they'll fish the oceans of the world clean."

I wanted to hear more about California and the lost men. But Father wouldn't tell me anymore. He took my hand and led me back to the house, and Mother stood on the porch and kissed me on the forehead and said dinner was almost ready.

We used to ride the horse to Grandfather's grave. It was up in a lot of brush. You couldn't get there in a car. I wondered why they buried him up there. Mother said it was the place he wanted to be buried. The grave was marked by a block of stone with his name carved on it.

We went to the grave for the last time a week before Jim was born. It hurt Mother to ride, but she said it didn't hurt enough to stop her from going.

Someone had stolen the headstone. Mother almost fell off the horse when she saw it was gone. We didn't even get down from the horse. She turned it and we rode back to the house as fast as the horse would go. Mother helped me get down and left me there. I watched her and the horse disappear across the fields. Father came back with her. She climbed off the horse, kneeled beside me and put her arms around me. When she stood, Father was gone.

I was lying in the dark that night, almost asleep, when I heard Father come back. After I woke up in the morning, Mother wouldn't talk about where he went. She said the baby was hurting her, and she wanted me to let her be.

"Old Jennings lives just down the road from the gravesite," Father told me that afternoon. "He saw strangers around there a couple of days ago." He turned away and talked to himself real low, resting one hand on the side of the house and looking at the fields.

Later, I heard him talking to Mother.

"Just because Jennings couldn't recognize them doesn't mean I can't find out who it was," he said. "Hell, Jennings is half-blind."

The next morning, I asked Father if it was Negroes. "Heck, boy," he said, "Jennings may have bad eyesight, but he can still tell white from black."

The demon is white, and I have no trouble seeing him in the dark. His eyes glow. He doesn't speak. He stands and stares until he climbs into the closet and Mother shakes my shoulder and I get up and we go out to the fields and pick strawberries. Sometimes we pick oranges. I like that better. When we stop working to eat our dinner, there's plenty of shade under the trees. Under the trees, the dirt is soft. But not as soft as in Oklahoma. And many of the other women smell funny.

Father smells funny after he comes home from work and washes the grease and oil from his hands and arms and gives the dirty clothes to Mother. I know if it's Sunday because Father doesn't go to work or smell. On Sunday he fixes the car he drives to work the rest of the week and we don't go to church anymore. But Mother says that doesn't matter.

"God watches us whether we go to church or not," she says. "He knows if we are worthy of Heaven. He watches and He knows." Then she groans and holds her stomach, since the new baby's hurting her, and I tell her to pray. She tells me we shouldn't pray for small things because it only angers God.

"I prayed when the wind came," she says. "But I shouldn't have. It was a test. When I die, the test will be at an end."

Jim was born before the wind came. One day, Mother cried out in the kitchen. I ran inside and she said she'd better go to the bedroom and lie down. She said "Go get your Father."

I ran across the fields and told him Mother wanted him. He ran back to the house ahead of me and went inside. Before I reached the house, he was back outside and cinching the saddle onto the horse. While I watched, he rode down the road.

There were tears in Mother's eyes, but she smiled at me from the bed.

"He's gone to get Mrs. Wilkins," she said. Her voice was strange. It was high and quick. "She's the one that was here for you. She's the one that was there for every baby in this county." Mother held my hand. Every now and then she squeezed it, and said "It won't be long now, Joe, it won't be long." She stopped speaking and squeezed my hand again and groaned. "It won't be long," she said, sounding lonesome and afraid.

Father came back in a car. It wasn't Mrs. Wilkins who was with him, but a man, a young man with a funny way of talking.

"Mrs. Wilkins is sick," Father told her. "She's got rheumatism so bad she can't raise her arms. This is the new doctor from town. He was visiting Mrs. Wilkins. It's a lucky thing for us he was already out this way."

"No," Mother said, talking loudly. "No. I can't have it, don't you see, Mrs. Wilkins is the one and you're a stranger, you and those others, come here and--"

Father took my hand and led me from the room and closed the door behind us.

"Go out and unhitch the mule from the plow and bring her in and feed her and close up the barn," he said. Then he opened the door, and Mother was sweating and moaning, and the doctor was standing over her, and Father closed the door. I unhitched the mule and put her in the barn. It was almost dark when I finally got her fed, since she wouldn't always move when I wanted her to.

No one came out of the room. I sat in the kitchen, put my head on the table top and fell asleep. When I woke up, Father was standing before me, holding the new baby. Father said his name was Jim.

"Why'd you name him Jim?" I said.

"That was your Grandfather's name." He said I wouldn't be able to see Mother for a while. She was sick. The doctor stayed for a long time. He ate supper with us. Father fixed it. He didn't go out to the fields all day. He stayed in the house and went in and out of the bedroom. After dark, the doctor got into his car and left. The next morning, Father let me see Mother.

She was lying in bed, with Jim next to her. She didn't have any color in her face, but she tried to smile. I asked her why she looked so pale.

"She's not pale," Father said.

Mother began to sob, and Jim began to cry, and I cried. Father stood over in a corner, looking out the window. He was whispering. He whispered all that afternoon. "Damn doctor," he whispered. "Goddamn doctor."

We had a horse in Oklahoma. If we had a horse now, it would scare the demon away. Me and Jim and Mother could ride it to where the strawberries grow. If we had a horse, we could get rid of the car. Father could ride the horse to work. I bet the demon is scared of horses. There wasn't hardly any sign of him before the wind killed the horse.

Not even Father knew the wind was coming. We were eating supper. Jim was too small to eat. He was in the bedroom, sleeping in his crib. We were eating when the sky got dark, and the wind began, sweeping across the fields and rattling over the house, shaking the windows. The noise woke Jim up. He began to cry, and I began to cry. Mother said "Hush!"

Father turned his head this way and that. He didn't say anything, but went outside. When he came back and slammed the door shut behind him, there was dirt all in his hair and on his face and clothes.

"Pray to God it doesn't last more than a day or so," he said to Mother. "Otherwise, there won't be an inch of topsoil left within a hundred miles of here."

But the wind didn't stop. It went on and on, for days and days, and for days and days Mother and Jim and me didn't leave the house and Father didn't plow. He'd pace back and forth with a strange look in his eyes. Once, I went into the bedroom and he was sitting in a corner by himself with his head in his hands. It scared me to see him like that.

When the wind finally stopped, everything had changed. The dirt was gone. Only sand remained. The sand was everywhere. It had gotten inside the house and the barn and the well.

Father took me out to the barn and I helped him walk the horse and the mule. They'd gone half-crazy because of the wind. I could hear them from the house, even above the rattling, kicking at the walls of the barn and crying out. Sometimes they did it all night. It scared me almost as much as the demon. He'd begun standing over the end of the bed. I tried to tell Father about it, while he led the horse and I led the mule in a circle in the sand before the barn. Father acted like he didn't hear me. He kept staring out over the fields and the sand. He had a strange look in his eyes, the look he has now when he smells funny. But he didn't smell then. He just stopped every once in a while and looked out at the fields until I asked him if the wind was over.

"No," he said, slow and deep. His throat must have been dry.

"How do you know?"

He looked down and watched me. Then he raised his hand and slapped me across the face.

"I know, goddamn it!" he said while I held back my tears. "Don't you sass me. I know."

It did come again, even worse than before. The wind and sand and dust slammed into the house. It blotted out the sun and went on into the night. When me and Jim went to bed the sand crashed against the window. When Mother woke me up it whistled and crashed, and the demon stood in the room all night and Father began to smell.

Mother had stopped praying. She saw me kneeling next to the bed one night before I went to sleep. She pulled me up and said "Don't, Joe. It's all a test. God would be angry for you to pray over such a little thing." So I prayed to myself. I prayed that the wind would stop. After it didn't, I stopped praying too and waited for the test to end. It couldn't last much longer, I thought. There wasn't hardly anything left to the farm.

Then the horse died. It was late at night. I couldn't sleep because of the demon and the wind, so I lay there a long time. I heard the horse and the mule, kicking at the barn's walls and crying out. The kicking stopped for a while, and it started again. I heard Mother, sobbing, and Father told me to get dressed and light the lantern.

We stepped out into the wind and opened the barn door. The mule ran past us and almost knocked me down. Father took the lantern and went inside. The horse was laying there. It didn't move or make a sound. Its eye was open but it had no life in it. Father bent over and felt its head and then its neck.

"It's broke," he said as he laid his hands on its neck. He stood and stared at the horse for a long time. Finally he turned and we went back to the house through the dust and sand. I climbed back in bed. While Mother cried, the demon came out of the closet and stood over the bed and watched me. His eyes glowed almost as bright as the lights on the front of the car Father bought to take us to California.

Mother wanted to visit Grandfather's grave before we left. The wind wasn't so bad anymore and I thought we would. We tried to, but the road was narrow and the car got stuck. It was stuck in a big rut and it rocked back and forth. All our things that were tied to the top of the car started falling on the ground.

"I'm turning back," Father said.

"No," Mother said. "It's just a little farther."

"Hell if it is," Father said. "Another five miles, at least."

"We can walk," she said. "It won't take any time."

"What--and leave everything we own setting in the open to be stolen or blown away?"

"No," Mother said. "I'm not moving until I've seen it."

Suddenly Father slapped her. Jim began crying, and I began crying, and tears came to Mother's eyes. But she didn't cry. When Father got the car out of the rut, he turned it around.

THE SCIENTIFIC METHOD

Four decades ago, Neil Young sang that Mother Nature was on the run. I don't know if Old Neil's heard the news, but she's returned--and with a vengeance.

As I walk towards Joshua Tree National Park on my morning constitutional, the driveways of the houses I pass all have something in common. The hood of every car and pick-up truck is raised. At first, I didn't understand what I was seeing. Why had all the vehicle owners done the same inexplicable thing?

Late one afternoon, I asked my neighbor what was going on.

"That's right," he replied. "You wouldn't know."

"Know what?" I said, a little impatiently.

"About the rats. They've been making everyone's lives miserable--crawling into engine compartments and chewing up the wiring. In one night, they'll disable a car."

He looked up and down the road. "Most of the houses around here don't have garages. Come sundown, the rats can go after almost any vehicle in the neighborhood."

He paused, watching me.

"You have a garage to park your Mazda in. That's why you don't know about all this trouble."

"What does popping the hoods open have to do with the rats?" I said.

"Everyone thinks they'll stay away if you raise your hood. Maybe the rats like their privacy." He shook his head. "But I learned the hard way that keeping the hood up isn't enough. When that's all I did, they caused over seven-hundred dollars in damage to my Chevy."

He raised his hand and tapped his index finger against the side of his head.

"That's when I turned to the scientific method," he said. "Observe and experiment. Come over here and I'll show you what I mean."

He led me to the Chevrolet Impala, parked under a carport in his driveway with its hood raised.

"Just before sundown, I use what I've learned through the scientific method to rat-proof this little beauty," he explained, patting his open palm gently on the car's fender. "The rats are nocturnal, you know. So I've got to finish my preparations before it gets dark."

He pointed towards the front of the Chevy. Its front tire was surrounded by rat traps. "They get to the engine by climbing up the tires and into the wheel wells. So the first thing I do is set these traps. Six traps per tire--twenty-four traps all together."

He motioned for me to stick my head under the hood. "Next, I soak mothballs with Pine-Sol and place them in as many of the engine block's nooks and crannies as I can reach. Finally, I take this solar light that I've been charging all day in the yard and set it on top of the air filter housing."

"And this keeps them away?"

"Works like a charm. Of course, it takes some time to put these defenses in place every afternoon. But it's time well spent."

A few weeks later, I was about to start my morning walk when I came upon my neighbor, standing before the Impala and staring down at the engine. He was cursing under his breath.

"Good morning," I said.

"Speak for yourself," he answered shortly. "Take a look at this."

In the midst of the mothballs was what appeared to be a pile of debris.

"They were here last night, building a nest," he said. "And now the car won't start."

My neighbor wasn't the only one who was formulating and testing hypotheses in an effort to stop the rats. That had become the main occupation among the regulars sitting around the horseshoe-shaped bar on Friday nights at the Twentynine Palms Inn.

"I heard the little fuckers don't like the smell of those softener sheets that people use in their dryers," noted the building contractor.

The man at the end of the bar who tracked the local tortoise populations for the Federal government guffawed lowly.

"My roommate covered his engine with 'em. Guess what the rats did?"

"Built a nest!" the blonde medical technician next to him shouted.

"What about these high-frequency sound wave machines they sell on the internet?" asked the retired Marine, scratching at his clean-shaven skull.

"I know a lady in Wonder Valley who paid thirty-five bucks for one," the man with long hair and lots of skull tattoos replied. "The first night she set it out, the rats chewed through the power cord."

Besides trying to discover a variation of the "loft-your-hood" remedy that worked, the townsfolk struggled to answer a fundamental question: Where did the rats come from?

"They don't belong here, I can tell you that," said my barber. "We've got our own rats out here, sure. But they're cute rats--kinda resemble little kangaroos. These new rats are big and ugly. They look like they belong in New York City."

There's a Marine base right next to the town. As the attacks on the vehicles spread, a rumor started that the rats had lived there for years but fled when the new commanding general launched an eradication effort. Suspicions existed, too, that the rats escaped from a secret government program on the base to create a Super Rat for use against the country's enemies around the world.

As another troubadour named Bob Dylan once sang: Something's happening but you don't know what it is.

Yesterday, I noticed that a crew of workers were demolishing the carport in front of my neighbor's house.

"What's going on?" I asked him.

He looked at me. "The scientific method tells me I need to build a garage," he said.

HISTORY IN THE MAKING

On July 21, 1969, they had their last fight. "You don't love me," she said, glaring into his narrow brown eyes. "You love the money I make and the gin and tequila I pay for. It's always about you, not us."

He stalked out to the street, climbed onto the Norton Commando, stomped his boot down on the shifter and watched the apartment's empty porch disappear in the rear view mirror.

She's right, he told himself as the motorcycle sped down the road's scorching asphalt, past bus stops, gas stations and supermarkets. She had him figured out. And that meant it was over.

The streets of Laguna Beach were jammed with visitors from Norwalk and Riverside searching for parking and deliverance from the summer heat. He found a crescent-shaped patch of sand at the edge of the seashore and laid on his back in his blue jeans and T-shirt and boots in the midst of all those bikinis and bare feet and Speedos.

She was the best thing he'd ever had, cute and smart and gentle. But he had worn out even her patience.

"I'll never forget this day," he muttered aloud. "The worst fucking day of my life."

While he stared through his sunglasses into the merciless sun, the strangers around him took no notice. Here and there, some of them also raised their faces to gaze overhead. But mostly, they were listening, transfixed, to their little transistor radios.

It was July 21, 1969, and up there, 238,900 miles past the cloudless blue sky, Neil Armstrong had just stepped onto the surface of the moon.

THE DAY THAT JOHN PAUL II WAS SHOT

The portly, middle-aged contractor was growing angrier by the second.

"No one else told me the rough grading certification would hold up my building permit," he barked impatiently as his ruddy cheeks grew redder. "What are you trying to do, drive me out of business? I'm paying a half-dozen guys to sit on their asses at the construction site and twiddle their thumbs. All because of a technicality."

He leaned forward. "If you worked in the real world, you'd know this red tape does nothing but cost people like me lots of money."

The lanky bureaucrat standing on the other side of the long wooden counter pressed his thin lips tightly together as he listened.

"I've got to get that permit this afternoon," the contractor muttered lowly. He sounded as though he was at the end of his rope. "Give me a break. I'll bring you the certification first thing tomorrow."

In an emotionless monotone, the younger man said: "There's nothing I can do. We're not in the habit of playing favorites here at the building department."

"Every other parcel in that subdivision is already built out," the contractor sputtered. His anger had returned. "There's no problem with the soil out there. You know that as well as I do."

"The permit won't be issued until I have the grading certification."

For a moment longer, the contractor glared at Roger. Then he snatched his briefcase from the counter's surface and silently stalked out the lobby's double glass doors.

The department's receptionist handed Roger a stack of phone messages as he walked by her desk. Pausing to glance down and flip through the slips of paper, he saw that one of them was from his wife.

"That guy's a tough customer," the attractive brunette said with an impish grin.

Roger raised his head. "Didn't you hear what he said? First thing tomorrow morning, he'll be here with the certification." He paused. "And that's when he'll get his permit."

He disappeared into a small, windowless room, empty except for a desk and chair, reached down for the phone and dialed his wife's work number.

"New accounts, Marge speaking."

"It's me."

"Oh. Hi, honey."

"Why'd you call?"

"The Pope's been shot," she announced breathlessly.

"What are you talking about?" he snapped.

"It's on the radio. Someone fired six shots while he was being driven through the crowds in St. Peter's Square."

He shook his head. "Who would want to shoot the Pope?"

"No one seems to know yet. Sorry, but I've got to go. I'll try and call you this afternoon. Don't forget to say a prayer for the Pope."

After he'd replaced the phone on its cradle, Roger fumbled in his trouser pocket until his fingertips touched the beads of his rosary.

He was in the midst of reciting a "Hail Mary" when the phone rang, startling him.

"Someone's here with a question about a residential patio cover," the receptionist told him.

A man with blonde hair, wearing a dark blue business suit and a red and beige striped tie, was waiting.

"Your standard patio cover plan says I have to provide a three foot wide catwalk next to any adjacent second floor bedroom window," the homeowner said, keeping his eyes on Roger. "Problem is, that catwalk's going to look like hell."

"It's required by the building code. Otherwise, there's no way for someone to safely escape through the bedroom window during an emergency such as a fire."

The man continued to stare at Roger. "Guess what? My cover's not going to have a catwalk," he announced.

"Then it's not going to have a building permit, either. Go ahead and build it anyway." Roger's voice grew louder, and he no longer spoke in a monotone. "Why should I care about your patio cover? The world's going crazy today. I don't know if you've heard. Somebody just shot the Pope. But see what happens when you try to sell the house in a few years and the buyer finds out the cover's illegal. You'll be right back here, begging for my help."

He turned and began walking towards his office. That's when a voice called from behind him.

"Wait a minute, goddamn it! We can work this out. I'm a law abiding citizen."

A slight smile, a smile that celebrated the fact that some things were still right with the world, flashed for a mere split second across Roger's features. This happened so quickly that the brunette couldn't be sure that she'd seen it.

Then he turned his usual poker face to the man at the counter.

SOMEONE ELSE TO LOVE

I'm writing to you from the past. When I'm finished, I plan to conceal this message in a way that'll prevent it from being found for many years. It's important for those of you who come after us to know the truth about the plague time.

By the fifth year of the pandemic, the world had become an entirely different place. Sources of factual information all but disappeared, though the unburied corpses littering vacant lots, farmers' fields and city alleys spoke for themselves. Everyone who was left alive had lost most of their loved ones. A song that was everywhere on what remained of the internet told the horrific tale:

It was God's almighty plan
To judge the wickedness
Of this old land
North and south
East and west
The virus did its best
To kill the rich
Kill the poor
And it's gonna keep killing
And then kill some more

No one could say why God brought this judgment down on us. Some claimed they knew, but their reasoning was wrapped up in what now seemed the petty issues from days gone by.

"It was because our courts allow abortion," said some.

"Because thousands of poor immigrant children were taken from their parents by the government and made orphans," claimed others.

Perhaps it was simply because we didn't love each other enough.

But five years of plague convinced the survivors to give up on love. They decided the only way to stay alive was to cut off contact with other human beings. Families split apart and went their separate ways. Priests abandoned their congregations. Politicians and rock stars lost their followers. Nurses deserted their patients.

For many, living alone came to mean living in a motor vehicle. It was a way to insure minimum contact with others while allowing for movement about the ravished landscape. Soon all the cars, trucks, vans, RVs and buses with running engines were snapped up.

I got my hands on a 1990's-era Lincoln Town Car. The thing's sheer bulk made it perfect for taking cuts in the hours-long lines at the few open gas stations. And the back seat was so spacious that it almost felt like I was sleeping in a bed. In fact, there was enough room back there for two. But a single casual sexual encounter could lead to a slow, agonizing death at the hands of the virus. Better to live another day and perform the rattlesnake shake as I lay alone in the dark.

The Lincoln was serving me well until the afternoon I raced through an empty residential neighborhood and missed seeing the hump of the concrete speed bump ahead of me. The low-riding car's oil pan scrapped over the top of it. Within a few blocks, the dashboard's warning light was glowing a brilliant red.

When I stepped out of the Lincoln, a stream of black oil had already begun flowing down the street and into the nearest gutter.

I had no tools--much less the mechanical skills to use them. Before the pandemic arrived, I was a junior copywriter at an advertising agency. My skill set seemed useless now. I lived day-to-day, confronting each new challenge as best I could. But avoiding the virus without an operating vehicle might spell the end of my feeble, stuttering attempt to stay alive.

I'd walked about two miles from the disabled Lincoln when the sun began to set. All around me were boarded-up storefronts. I wished I'd stayed with the car. At least I'd have someplace to sleep.

That's when I heard the cry.

"Hello there!"

I jerked my head this way and that, scanning the abandoned downtown in search of the source. Another human was calling to me. And another human meant possible infection.

"Up here!"

The voice, which sounded like it belonged to an excited child, was close by.

Suddenly I spotted a face, smiling down at me from an open second story window on the opposite side of the street. Not the face of a child, but that of a young woman about my age.

"I haven't seen anyone in weeks," she shouted. "What's your name?"

I didn't answer. For years, I'd been avoiding human contact. Responding to her question went against everything I knew about surviving. As I silently watched, I could see her smile disappear.

"Johnny," I replied, not really understanding what had come over me. "My name's Johnny. What's yours?"

"Laura." Her smile returned. "What brings you here?"

"My car stopped running."

"I'll be down in a minute."

Before I could object, she disappeared. In a few seconds, a door on the building's first floor swung open and she stepped out into the twilight. Tall and slim, she wore a simple shift with colorful prints of butterflies all over it.

"Stay where you are!" I demanded.

She stopped in her tracks. "I haven't seen anyone in weeks."

"You already told me that. Keep your distance." I sighed. "I don't mind talking to you. But I intend to keep on living."

She stared at me. Even in the fading light, I could see that tears were beginning to roll down her freckled cheeks.

"Do you call this living?" she gasped.

I only had one answer. "It beats the alternative," I said.

Wiping the tears from her eyes, she sputtered: "Do you really believe that?"

Then she began walking towards me. This time, I didn't try to stop her. She extended her hand. I took it and pulled her closer, until we were face-to-face.

The last time I'd been this close to a woman was years before, when my parents announced it was best if they, my younger brother and I all went our separate ways. Before my father could stop her, my mother took me in her arms and pressed her cheek against mine.

I nodded towards the second floor window as I held on to her hand. "Do you live up there?"

"Yes. Want to see?"

I'd already touched her. What difference did it make now if we were in her room together? Besides, she seemed to be healthy.

At the top of a flight of stairs, I followed her through an open doorway and into a tiny apartment.

"This is my place," she said, watching me.

The only furnishings were a narrow bed and a metal desk with a beat-up wooden chair beside it. The room's walls were lined with plastic bags.

"Those hold everything I own in the world," she noted. "Make yourself comfortable." She pointed at the edge of the bed and switched on a pole lamp in the corner. "I'll bring you some tea."

When she returned from the kitchen with two cups, she sat next to me. As night fell, we shared the experiences that everyone our age had been through because of the pandemic. Such as learning there were no longer going to be schools. And realizing that your best friends had all died.

After a while, we stood and went to the window where I'd first seen her. The street below was dark and empty. But above us, the Big Dipper filled the blackness of the sky.

Not everything has changed, I thought.

"I have to go. I need to find my car," I told her. "I'll come back tomorrow. I want to see you again."

She grasped my elbow.

"Stay here tonight," she said.

Without a word, we took each other in our arms.

From that evening on, we were inseparable. For the first few days, we did little more than make love on the tiny bed and sleep. On the third day, though, we began to do the things that were required to survive. This meant scavenging through the abandoned town for anything valuable enough to trade for food.

Out in the countryside, two brothers who refused to part had started a farm. From a distance, we'd hold up what we had to barter and they'd shout back the names of the vegetables that were in season. They told us about a childhood friend of theirs who was a hunter. Thanks to him, we had a regular supply of rabbit and squirrel.

One night at the window, we noticed a fire in the distance. The next day, I discovered it was my Lincoln. Nothing remained except a smoldering metal skeleton.

It wasn't long after that when I was awakened in the middle of the night by the sound of her gasping for breath. Somehow, she had caught the virus.

As her condition worsened, she urged me to leave her. "The longer you stay, the more chance there is that you'll get infected too. I want you to keep on living."

"I don't want to live without you," I said.

She stared at me. "Don't be silly," she replied impatiently.

I leaned forward and kissed her. "You're the one who's being silly," I said.

She passed away a week ago. We'd talked about where I should bury her. After she was gone, I carried her body to the place she'd chosen at the top of a ridge above the town. She and I also discussed this message I'm writing to you. We both felt it was important for you to know that some of us retained our humanity. That some of us continued to love one another.

I've packed up my belongings and soon will be on my way. First, I'll take this message, place it in a metal music box that her parents gave her when she was ten years old and bury it next to her unmarked grave. Then I'll follow the empty highway--and pray with each step that I find someone else to love.

TOO MANY EMPTY HEARTS

January 13, 1955

"Mom, I have to talk with you."

The woman looked up from the kitchen counter, where she'd just begun seasoning a lump of ground beef for that evening's meatloaf dinner. Her oldest daughter's face wore a worried look.

"What is it, Connie?"

"Mary came to me a little while ago." She hesitated before going on. "She thinks she's pregnant."

Mrs. LaCross squinted at the teenager.

"Pregnant?" she repeated, disbelief in her tone. "She's only fifteen. Did she tell you who the father is?"

"Clarence, that boy who works at the gas station. What are we going to do, Mom?"

The woman sighed as she wiped her hands on her apron. Then she marched out of the kitchen and down the hallway that led to the rest of the house. Mary's bedroom door was closed. Without knocking, she pushed it open.

Her younger daughter looked up from where she sat on the edge of her bed, in the midst of folding a stack of freshly washed blouses.

"Do I have to marry Clarence?" she muttered timidly.

"Find your rosary," her mother commanded, "and pray to the Virgin Mary for forgiveness."

Later that afternoon, Mary's father arrived home from work and he, Mrs. LaCross and Connie huddled at the kitchen table while the meatloaf baked in the oven.

Soon the door to Mary's room swung open again. "Come with me," Connie told her sister.

Back in the kitchen, they joined their parents.

"You're a great disappointment to the Lord, and to us," the man said. "If anyone else in this town finds out what's happened, it would disgrace our family and our parish."

He glared into Mary's eyes.

"But they are never going to find out."

March 15, 1980

John LaCross stood in the hallway, knocking loudly on the apartment's metal door. Earlier that morning, he'd dialed Sharon's number several times. But her phone seemed to be out of order.

He was ready to give up and leave when he decided to try the doorknob. It turned in his hand.

Once inside, he glanced around the tiny apartment. There was no one to be seen. It was then that he noticed the photo on top of the TV. He picked up the eight-by-ten color print.

Sharon lay nude on her back, staring at the camera. Her blonde hair framed her narrow face and fell over her bare shoulders. He thought he saw a mix of fear and shame in her countenance.

"Where did this come from?" he wondered aloud.

He took the photo into the kitchen. The refrigerator was empty except for two cans of Schlitz. He popped one open.

As he studied the photo, he heard the front door creaking and raised his head.

Sharon stood in the doorway, holding a bulging paper supermarket sack against her chest. A short, stocky man with long black hair was beside her, staring angrily at John. He wore a T-shirt with cut-off sleeves that revealed tan and silver rattlesnake tattoos, coiling up both of his muscular arms. The snakes' eyes were red ink swastikas.

"Who're you?" he said, loudly and ominously.

John nodded at Sharon. "A friend of hers. What's it to you?"

Reaching into a pocket of his jeans, the man produced a Buck knife and unfolded its blade.

"I'm gonna hurt you," he promised. "Real bad."

"Rudy! Leave him alone!" Sharon pleaded.

"Shut up!" he growled.

John stepped back until he bumped against the wall behind him. He had nowhere else to go. When the man saw the surprise and confusion on his face, a cruel smirk crossed his lips.

As he watched Rudy, John's leg brushed against something beside him. He looked down to see a short baseball bat, the kind used by Little Leaguers, propped against the wall. Sharon had told him she kept it there in case the gang members who lived on the same floor tried to break into her place.

He snatched up the aluminum cylinder and held it in front of his chest. Now it would be all-but-impossible for the man to use the blade.

Rudy glared at him for a moment.

"Go to the pick-up and get my shotgun," he told Sharon.

The sack of groceries slipped out of her grasp and crashed onto the floor.

"Rudy...I...I can't," she stuttered as a chill ran up John's spine.

"Go on!" he shouted over his shoulder.

"I can't!" she insisted again, clutching her hands together.

He glanced her way. "If you don't get that shotgun," he said, "I'll kill you instead. I'll do it, bitch."

She slumped to the floor and, sobbing, covered her head with her arms.

"Shit!" Rudy hissed.

He turned towards her. As she cowered before him, he bent over and jabbed the knife savagely into the side of her body.

While John watched, the man disappeared out the doorway.

He kneeled beside her. She lay on her back, moaning and bleeding onto the floor. A crimson pool was already forming on the linoleum.

He looked about him, until he remembered her phone wasn't working. Rushing down the stairway to the street, he sprinted for several blocks before coming upon a public phone that hadn't been vandalized into uselessness. The operator connected him to the police department.

"My girlfriend's been stabbed," he said excitedly.

After he recited the apartment's address, the husky voice on the other end of the line asked: "What's your name, sir?"

John hung up the receiver.

A crowd had formed around the front of the apartment building by the time he returned. A red and white paramedic van was parked at the curb, roof lights flashing. Across the street were two black-and-white police cruisers.

At the edge of the group of onlookers, two elderly women stood together, speaking in hushed tones.

"I overheard a policeman say she's been seriously injured," whispered one of the women. Nervously, she tilted her head in John's direction. When she saw his face, a look of shock crossed her own features.

"It's him!" she shouted, pointing at John with a trembling finger. "The man who ran out of her apartment!"

A policeman suddenly appeared and firmly grasped John's arm.

"Are you sure?" the cop said.

"Yes!"

"Look, I was in her apartment," he admitted, "but I didn't touch her."

As he spoke, another policeman appeared and grabbed his free arm. In no time at all, the three of them were surrounded by the crowd.

"Let's take him upstairs," said the cop who'd just arrived.

"Right." The second policeman turned to the old woman. "Could you follow us?" he asked.

She hesitated. "I suppose so."

They pushed through the neighbors and climbed the building's grimy stairs. At the door to Sharon's second floor apartment, which was closed and guarded by another policeman, they stopped.

"Get Franklin," one of John's escorts told the cop at the door.

An overweight and balding man in a rumpled brown suit emerged and pulled the door shut behind him.

"What is it?" he asked the policemen as he gazed at John.

"This lady saw him run out of the apartment."

"She may have seen me," John said. "But you've got the wrong guy."

"Wait a minute." Franklin raised his hands. "Let's start from the beginning. Why were you at her place?"

"I was waiting for her to come home."

"Did you have a key?"

"No. The door was unlocked. A few minutes later, she showed up with another man, someone I'd never seen before. We got into an argument—"

"Who did?" said Franklin.

"This man and I," John answered impatiently. "He told her to go to his pick-up truck and bring back his shotgun. When she refused, he stabbed her and split."

"Why were you running out of the apartment?"

"To find a phone. Listen--why don't you ask Sharon what happened?"

"I wish I could," Franklin said. "She's dead."

The old woman pressed an open palm to her forehead. "Oh my God," she whispered.

"Dead?" John repeated as if in a daze.

While one of the cops escorted the distraught neighbor down the hallway to her apartment, Franklin turned to the remaining policeman.

"Put the cuffs on him," he ordered.

For a moment, John felt as if he was going to pass out. "I didn't do anything," he told Franklin as his hands were locked together.

The detective pulled a small, worn card from his coat pocket. "You're under arrest for the murder of Sharon Stanley," he said. He read John his rights from the card. Then they took him to the police station, which was located a few blocks away.

After he'd been booked, photographed and fingerprinted, a cop stood at John's side while he dialed his mother-in-law's number.

Mrs. Cassidy answered the phone.

"Is Amanda there?" he asked anxiously. "This morning she told me she was having lunch with you."

"She already went back to work."

"I know she's not allowed to take personal calls at her office," John said. "I need you to drive over there and give her a message. I've been arrested."

"Arrested?" the woman gasped.

"I'm at the Anaheim police station. Ask Amanda to get an attorney and come over here as soon as she can."

His wife arrived with Norman Stewart about ninety minutes later. The middle-aged man had represented Amanda's older brother two years before when he was arrested for selling marijuana. They sat across from John at a long counter with a pane of thick glass mounted at its center. The sound of her voice, amplified through a speaker that was mounted over John's head, startled him.

"We just talked to the detective," the small, attractive woman said. "This is horrible, John. How could they think that you..." Her voice trailed off.

The attorney opened a briefcase and produced a notepad.

"Let's go over a few things while events are still fresh in your memory."

Stewart asked him to explain what happened when Sharon and Rudy entered the apartment. As John described the stabbing, Amada covered her mouth with the fingers of one hand.

The attorney studied the scribble on the notepad. He raised his head.

"Why were you in her place?" he asked.

John looked at Amanda.

"She'll find out everything sooner or later," Stewart said.

He kept his eyes on his wife. "I was having an affair with her."

"How long had this been going on?" Amanda asked.

He hesitated before answering.

"Three months."

He could see her eyes filling with tears.

"I need some fresh air," she said.

Stewart helped her to her feet.

"Amanda..." he whispered.

"We'll talk about this later," she told her husband. She and the attorney turned their backs on him and silently walked out of the room.

July 18

Rudy sat at the bar of the El Perro Negro cantina and ordered another shot of tequila. He gulped down the liquor and then scooted off the stool. The shadowy room was almost empty. Tomorrow was Friday, though—which meant Americans in RVs, pulling trailers loaded with dirt bikes through the dusty streets, would begin filling the small town. San Felipe had been founded on the fertile waters of the Gulf of California thirty years before by fishermen. But its proximity to the U.S. border and its wide beaches had transformed the place into a weekend getaway.

Rudy strolled through the blistering early evening heat towards the lights of the business district. He walked into a wood frame building with a crudely painted green sign above the doorway announcing FISH TACOS. Taking a seat at one of the restaurant's beat-up tables, he ordered a burrito and a Corona beer.

As he bit into a tortilla chip, Rudy thought about the murder. He felt no guilt over killing Sharon. In his mind, what happened was all her fault. But it had disrupted his plans. He'd intended to become a pimp. And she was to be his first whore.

"You're already screwing three or four guys a week," he'd told her. "You might as well get paid for it."

The nude photograph was his idea, a means of drumming up customers. Printing a hundred copies of the photo hadn't been cheap. Now he'd have to start over again. With another woman.

While he swallowed the last of the beer, Rudy watched two couples enter the restaurant. They held on to each other's shoulders for support as they bumped through the entrance. The young men looked like brothers; both were lanky, with sandy hair that hung in bangs over their tanned foreheads. One of the women was also slim. Her black hair was cut just above her shoulders. The second woman was a short, pudgy redhead whose large breasts were covered by a tight halter top.

One of the men knocked over the chair he was trying to pull out from under a table. It crashed to the floor. His companions were so drunk that they barely reacted to the racket. But Rudy raised his face in irritation.

"Asshole," he said loudly.

The man who toppled the chair stared angrily at Rudy with his bloodshot eyes.

"Fuck you," he muttered, slurring the words together.

Rudy was on him in seconds—landing a vicious uppercut to the jaw and, once he'd fallen heavily to the floor, kicking him violently in the ribs with his steel-toed boot. As the other drunks stared, wide-eyed, at their companion's crumpled body, Rudy brushed roughly past them and walked briskly away.

His motel was to the south of town, on the top of a hill. As he followed a narrow pathway past an overgrown wash, he heard a pair of voices.

He stopped and listened.

"Where'd you tell your mom you were going?" asked a boy. He sounded like he couldn't be older than thirteen or fourteen.

"To the liquor store to buy a Coke," said a teenage girl.

"Did she believe you?"

"Who cares! I hate her. Ever since my dad split, she's been a bitch."

"Just like my mom. You should've heard her and her new boyfriend last night."

"Whatta you mean?"

"They were at the other end of the trailer, grunting and groaning like a couple of hogs!"

The pair giggled in the dark.

"How come it's okay for them to fuck around, but it's not okay for us?" said the girl.

"Because they're full of shit."

Crazy world, Rudy thought to himself. Everyone's marriages are falling apart, children don't respect their parents. Everything's compromise.

The pair had grown silent. As he squinted into the wash, he made out their glistening eyes. They were watching him.

"Hey, pervert!" the boy shouted. "Whatta you looking at?"

Rudy descended awkwardly into the brush, slipping down the side of the wash as he went.

They sat next to one another in the darkness. Rudy grabbed the boy by his shoulder-length hair and pulled him to his feet.

"O-w-w!" he cried. "You fucking asshole!"

With his free hand, Rudy slapped him hard across the face.

"Shut up, shithead," he hissed into the boy's ear.

He stopped struggling then and Rudy let go of his hair.

"Take your little girlfriend and get outta here," he said. "And if you ever talk like that to me again, I'll cut your mother's throat."

They began running down the pathway towards the beach. When they'd reached the road, the boy stopped and turned towards Rudy.

"Fuck you!" he shouted. "YOU'RE the fucking shithead!"

For a moment, he almost went after them. He was so angry that his head had begun to throb painfully. But he knew he'd look like a crazy man, chasing two kids around in the night. As he stood there, he realized, too, that he'd be able to find the boy whenever he wanted. There weren't many places to hide in San Felipe.

Then he remembered the tequila in his room. By the time he was sitting on the edge of the bed, sucking at the end of the tilted bottle, his headache had almost disappeared.

August 25

The prosecutor's name was Joshua Kenney. The handsome man paced slowly back and forth in front of the jury as he delivered his opening remarks in the manner of an outraged fundamentalist preacher.

"The defendant had a problem," he noted, spreading his arms. "He was a married man with a girlfriend. His solution was to stab the girlfriend to death." He stared at the jurors and grasped his hands together. "What the State will prove," he intoned, "is that the defendant waited in his victim's apartment, drinking a beer, before he surprised her and plunged a knife into her cowering body."

The man's voice grew louder. "Ladies and gentlemen, I have just described the actions of a monster. And that is exactly what the State will prove—that John LaCross is a monster who should be executed for his hideous crime."

John glanced over his shoulder at the first row of spectators, where Amanda and a white-haired couple sat together. All three wore the same intense, pained expression. The old man held the beads of a rosary between the fingers of his right hand.

Norman Stewart stood in his turn to address the jury, which was composed of five men and seven women. Except for a secretary in her mid-twenties, a middle-aged building contractor and a bald man who owned a small plastics manufacturing firm, the jurors were all retirees in their sixties and seventies.

"John LaCross is like the rest of us," Stewart explained. "He has made mistakes in his life. He was having an affair with Sharon

Stanley. But he did not kill her. He happened to be in the wrong place at the wrong time."

Stewart outlined what took place in Sharon's apartment after she and Rudy arrived on the fateful morning. As he spoke, he stepped to the side of the jury box.

"It is up to the prosecution to prove that John was something more than a victim of circumstance." He paused for a long moment, looking into the eyes of one juror and then the next.

"The defense is confident this is an impossible task, because John LaCross is an innocent man."

September 1

As the second week of the trial began, Stewart saw that Amanda and the elderly couple once again sat in the first row.

"You have some very loyal supporters," he said.

John nodded. "Amanda's boss is letting her come in late so she can be here in the mornings."

"Are those your parents with her."

He stared at the attorney for a moment.

"Yes and no," he finally replied.

I wonder what that's supposed to mean, Stewart thought. But today he had more important things on his mind. The prosecution had called Sharon's neighbor to the witness stand.

"What did you do," Kenney asked, "after seeing the defendant flee the scene of the murder?"

"Well...I called the police. It...it seemed funny, the way that man"—she glanced uneasily at John—"ran out of Sharon's apartment."

"The defense claims another man was also in her apartment. Did you see anyone else besides Mr. LaCross?"

She shook her head. "No. No one else."

Kenney asked the old woman about encountering John later in the crowd at the entrance to the building.

"I nearly fainted," she said. "I looked up and he was standing right beside me." She paused. "I thought he'd come back to kill me for seeing him."

"Objection," Stewart said from his chair at the defense table.

"Sustained." The judge glanced at the court reporter. "Strike that last sentence," he instructed. The portly man turned to the jury. "That last remark is inadmissible," he told them. "It should be disregarded."

"I...I'm sorry," she said. "It's just that I was so frightened."

Stewart dropped his pencil on the table and let out a loud sigh.

When it was his turn to cross-examine, he stood in front of the woman.

"Were you in the hallway before the defendant left Sharon's apartment?" he asked.

"No, no," she said. "I was just going out when I noticed him ahead of me."

"Could someone else have left Sharon's apartment before you saw Mr. LaCross?"

She shrugged. "I don't know."

"That's possible, isn't it?"

The woman stared at him.

"Answer the question," the judge told her.

"If there was someone else," she said, "I think I would've seen them."

"I have several more questions," Kenney said, getting to his feet. "How long was Sharon your neighbor?"

"Oh, at least a year."

"During those twelve months, did you ever hear voices come from her apartment?"

"Sometimes, yes. The walls are thin."

Kenney took several steps towards the witness stand and stopped in front of the woman.

"Did you hear any voices on the day of Sharon's murder?"

"No," she said, shaking her head. "I didn't hear a thing."

"Are you sure you didn't hear the voices of two men in Sharon's apartment that day?"

She nodded. "I'm sure."

That afternoon, Amanda visited John at the Orange County Jail, an Orwellian concrete structure that rises out of downtown Santa Ana's barrio. The pair sat facing one another.

"It didn't go well today, did it?" he said. "I wish Stewart hadn't bothered cross-examining the neighbor."

She watched him without replying.

He pursed his lips. "I can't tell you how sorry I am. About everything."

"Let's concentrate on getting through the trial," she replied.

While she steered their silver Ford Fiesta out of the jail's parking lot and onto the street, she suddenly pulled the car to the curb. She had come to realize there was a very good chance he would be convicted. Learning of his affair with Sharon had hurt her deeply. But she was sure he was incapable of committing such a horrendous act.

She began to weep--for herself, and for him.

September 5

The morning light woke Rudy with a start. He glanced at the woman who lay sleeping beside him on the narrow bed. He'd picked her up the night before in a bar on the beach. After he'd asked if she wanted a drink, the rest happened so fast that he couldn't remember if she'd told him her name.

He shook her bare shoulder. "Get up," he commanded loudly.

She groaned and rubbed at her eyes with the backs of her hands. "What time is it?" she mumbled.

"How should I know?"

He went into the bathroom and took a piss. When he re-emerged, she was still in bed.

"Come on, get up," he told her again.

She pushed her long brown hair away from her hazel eyes. "What's your hurry?" she asked with a smirk, glancing at his limp penis.

He picked his jeans up from the floor and pulled them on.

"I've got lots of things to do today. But I want to see you again. Where you staying?"

She slipped on her bra as she spoke. "That trailer park across the road. My ex-husband was generous enough to let us use his trailer this summer. He's such a gentleman." Her tone dripped with sarcasm.

"I'll come by tonight."

She moved to the cracked mirror above the dresser. "I'd rather come here," she said as she brushed her hair.

"Why? You got someone staying with you?"

She put down the brush, moved to his side and grasped his elbow.

"My son's here, too. And he gets jealous. You know how boys are," she said, stroking the back of his thick neck.

Once she left, Rudy got down on all fours and pulled his shotgun, which was wrapped in a burlap sack, out from under the bed. Sitting in the room's only chair, he took the gun apart and cleaned it. He loved the smell of the grease and the feel of the hard, cold metal. The shotgun was the great equalizer; it could waste a cop, a rich man, anyone. If Sharon had only gone and gotten it for him. Although he realized it would probably never happen, Rudy hoped that, somehow, he'd cross paths with John LaCross again.

"That son of a bitch's put me through a lot of trouble," he said aloud, sighting down the gun's barrel. He was growing bored with his self-imposed Mexican exile. He hadn't found a replacement for Sharon to pimp out. And he was running low on money.

After reassembling the shotgun, he wrapped it in the sack again and pushed the bundle under the mattress. Then he pulled on his boots and walked out the door.

He ignored the bay's sparkling blue water. Walking towards town along the sandy road, he was trying to think of a way to come up with some cash. He'd already batted around the idea of robbing one of the liquor stores. The town was so small, though, that he'd have to kill every witness to insure he wasn't fingered later. Way too messy, he'd decided.

He walked into the first restaurant he came to. The place was empty except for two people: the divorcee who'd been his lover during the night and her son. They were sitting at a table, studying the mimeographed menus.

The woman smiled at him nervously as he sat down beside her.

"This your son?"

She nodded. "Tyler, this is Rudy."

The long-haired adolescent didn't answer, but held the menu in front of his face.

"What you gonna have?" Rudy asked her.

"Oh, I don't know. I'm getting tired of Mexican food."

"How about you, Tyler?"

The boy continued to hide behind the menu.

"You like Mexican food?" Rudy said.

"It's okay," he mumbled.

At the sound of his voice, Rudy frowned. He realized now why the boy kept his features covered.

"I hope they have a restroom here," she said before disappearing down a hallway.

Rudy leaned across the table.

"You remember me?"

"No," the teenager answered impatiently, still concealed.

"I think you do." Rudy paused. "I told you I'd cut your mother's throat if you ever talked to me again. So you ran down the hill and called me a fucking shithead."

"You know what I'm gonna do? Keep my promise. Tonight."

He continued to look towards the boy. "I'll be doing you a favor, dude. My mother was just like her. Always hooking up with men who didn't give a shit about her—or me. When I was about your age, she dumped me off on a street corner. That was the last time I ever saw her. She chose a guy she'd met the night before over her own son. Her own flesh and blood."

"Yeah, you'll be better off once the bitch is buried in the ground."

When Tyler's mother reappeared, Rudy stood. "I'm not that hungry. I'll see you tonight," he told her.

As he walked to the doorway, he looked over his shoulder. Tyler had set down the menu and was watching him. He winked at the teenager.

That afternoon as he emerged from El Perro Negro, he saw the woman and her son pulling out of the trailer park in a battered orange VW. The rear seat of the small car was piled high with suitcases and backpacks. She purposely ignored him as she drove past. While Rudy watched, Tyler stuck his scrawny arm out the passenger window and flipped him off.

After the VW had gone, he considered following the pair into the desert that separated San Felipe from the U.S. border and forcing them off the road. But there was always the possibility that someone might happen along. Still, the image of the boy's hand, with its middle finger raised defiantly in the air, was almost unbearable. Rudy's head began to throb so painfully that he almost tripped over his own feet as he returned to the bar.

"Back already?" said the bartender.

"Give me a shot of tequila."

He yanked the full glass out of the man's grasp, threw back his head and gulped down the clear liquid.

"You want another?" the bartender asked.

"Fuck you!" Rudy shouted. He flung the glass across the room and stalked out the door.

The bartender shook his balding head as he watched the man disappear into the sunlight.

"Crazy son of a bitch," he muttered.

September 6

Every Saturday morning since John's arrest, Amanda and Stewart met for breakfast. It was an opportunity for the attorney to review the status of the trial, describe what he expected would happen in the coming weeks and answer her questions.

On this particular morning, though, it was Stewart who had a question.

"I asked John if the couple who sit with you in the courtroom are his parents. I didn't understand his answer. He said 'yes and no.' What do you think he meant?"

She set down her cup of coffee.

"John's mother, Mary, was only fifteen when she became pregnant with him. Her parents didn't want anyone to know what had happened. They're strict Catholics, and thought the pregnancy and birth of the illegitimate child would cast shame on the family—and the Church. So Mary and her older sister, Connie, moved to another town with their mother until he was born. Everyone outside of the immediate family was told the new baby was Mary's brother.

"For most of his life, John thought his grandmother was his mother. And thought his mother was his sister. Three years ago, Mary died in a traffic accident. That's when Connie told John the truth."

Stewart shook his head. "That must have shocked the hell out of him."

She pushed her lips tightly together.

"It completely changed our relationship—for the worst. He didn't trust me any longer. And I suspected that he'd started seeing other women." She paused. "Unfortunately, I was right."

She watched the attorney.

"He's not the same man I married."

September 7

Norman Stewart and his companion didn't fit in. Their business suits contrasted sharply with the overalls, plaid shirts and blue jeans of the other customers who sat beside them at the little diner's counter. The pair stirred their coffees while the white-smocked cook fried a dozen patties at once.

"Best burgers in Orange County," Stewart said.

The second man, whose name was Felix, nodded. His long black hair was tied into a ponytail that hung over his tight collar. The man seemed too large for his clothes. In fact, he barely fit on the stool.

Stewart pulled a black and white photocopy from his coat pocket and set it between them on the counter top. Printed on the paper was the nude picture of Sharon.

"The original's a color print," he said as Felix examined the picture. "Think you can find the photo shop that printed this? It's important. Very important."

"What can you tell me about it?"

"The woman's dead."

"A prostitute?"

"Could be." Stewart paused. "The print may have been ordered by a man named Rudy."

"What was her name?"

"Sharon Stanley."

Felix raised his head and Stewart met his stare.

"You're always telling me you want the interesting cases," the attorney noted.

At that moment, the waitress set a plate in front of each of them. She tried to catch a glimpse of the photo, but the big man jealously snatched it up.

"You know what I think of John LaCross," he said after she'd left them.

Stewart shifted on his stool. "I do. And I think LaCross is telling the truth."

"Assume I find the lab where this photo came from. What if the print was ordered by LaCross?" the detective asked.

Stewart shrugged. "Then I'll switch to Plan B. After I figure out what the hell Plan B is."

September 11

Over the previous four days, Felix had visited a dozen photo labs. No luck. Most of the clerks and technicians simply glanced at the photocopy of the nude woman and shook their heads. One man asked, with a grin, if he could have Sharon's phone number. Another man grew angry. "Get out of here!" he demanded. "I don't deal in pornography."

The big man sighed as he sat in his black Lincoln Continental and flipped through the phone book. He thought LaCross was guilty as sin. It was an open-and-shut case. But Stewart believed John's cockamamie alibi. And Stewart was paying his invoices.

"What a way to make a living," he muttered as he closed the yellow pages and started the Lincoln's engine.

On a narrow, rundown street, Felix parked before a tiny wood frame house. "Darkroom. Photo Enlarging" announced a small sign that was mounted in a window at the front of the building.

Just inside the doorway, a short Chicano in his early twenties stood behind a makeshift plywood counter.

"You the owner?" Felix asked.

"Whatta you need?"

He set the photocopy of Sharon on the counter's top. "You recognize this? The original was a color print."

The young man glanced at the photo.

"Yeah, I remember this job. Who wouldn't. Nice tits, huh?" He paused. "You a cop?"

"No. A private investigator. Who ordered the print?"

"Who wants to know?"

The detective pulled out his wallet and placed a twenty dollar bill next to the photo.

"Who ordered the print?" he asked again.

"You mean prints, as in lots more than one."

The clerk reached beneath the counter and produced a shoebox full of yellow receipts. Quickly thumbing through the papers, he soon found what he was looking for.

Felix took the receipt from his hand. It was for one-hundred color prints. They'd been ordered five months before by "Rudy" and were paid for in cash. The receipt listed no phone number or address for the customer.

"Where's Rudy live?" the big man said as he tapped his knuckles on top of the twenty dollar bill.

"How should I know? But you won't have a problem telling if you found your man. He's a piece of work. Built like a fire plug. With snake tattoos and swastikas all over his arms."

That afternoon, the detective phoned Stewart and related what he'd learned. "You were right about LaCross," he admitted. "Good thing we didn't bet on it."

"I wouldn't do that to you," the attorney said. "Not after taking you to the cleaners in Caliente last year."

"Your luck'll run out sooner or later. Then I'll get you," Felix said, his voice rising. "I'll win every single penny back. Every fucking cent."

September 20

Outside, sunlight filled the sky. Billowing white clouds hung above the eastern horizon in mile-long banks. Gulls swept over the calm blue and green surface of the Sea of Cortez. And fishermen called to one another from their skiffs as they tossed their nets into the water.

The beauty of the day was lost on the half-dozen men who sat in the eternal shadows of the Club Miramar. They were busy watching the blonde who'd just staggered through the swinging doors. She sat at the long oak bar in her tight purple shorts and ordered a double gin and tonic.

Someone went to the jukebox. Dropping in several quarters, he pushed the machine's colorful illuminated buttons. A slow blues filled the place, eternal and mournful. Then Mick Jagger began to sing the tale of how an empty heart is like an empty life.

The shirtless American, who wore cut-off jeans and flip flops, moved from the jukebox to the blonde.

"Wanna dance?" he asked.

She looked up at him. Although her face was caked with make-up, the wrinkles still showed through.

"Okay."

As soon as she'd gotten off the stool, he pulled her close to him. They almost tripped over each other's feet as they slowly circled the empty dance floor.

"...An empty heart..." Jagger moaned.

Rudy sat alone beside the jukebox, watching the couple pass. He picked up the shot glass and gulped down the mezcal. A feeling of sadness filled his soul. He was weary of long days and nights in friendless rooms, of the loneliness that inevitably returned to follow the sour taste of too much alcohol.

Across the room, two bearded men with cowboy hats on their heads guffawed loudly. "Get it on!" one of them shouted, grinning at the slow motion dancers.

When the song ended, the couple sat next to one another at the bar.

Another song began as the bartender placed a round of drinks in front of them. The man who'd shouted at the pair pulled his hat down over his forehead and got to his feet. His boots clumped on the scarred dance floor as he went over to the woman and tapped her on the shoulder. When she turned, he wordlessly grasped her ample waist with both hands and pulled her off the stool.

She nearly fell on her face, but he steadied her and wrapped his arms around her neck.

"You're just the woman to fill my empty heart," he whispered in her ear as they, too, awkwardly circled the room.

Rudy stared at the shot glass. He couldn't afford to buy another drink—not even rotgut mezcal. He'd planned on returning to Orange County weeks ago. But the trial was going on longer than he'd anticipated.

When the song ended, he slipped out of the booth and walked outside. He cursed under his breath as he considered his dilemma. Staying in San Felipe until LaCross had been convicted was the smart thing to do. But he couldn't remain in Mexico any longer without money. The rent on the motel room was already a week overdue.

On the next block, two women wearing large straw hats stood under a canvas sunshade and picked through piles of embroidered blouses, stacked neatly on a card table.

"Find any bargains?" Rudy asked, stopping behind them.

The taller of the two glanced at him. She was in her early twenties, with long red hair, bright blue eyes and a complexion like alabaster.

"Not yet," she answered indifferently.

As he took a step closer, Rudy suddenly froze in his tracks. A transparent plastic purse hung off her shoulder. Inside of it, his own face stared cruelly from the front page of the Santa Ana Register.

He began walking very quickly towards the motel.

The manager, a barrel-chested man with salt-and-pepper hair that he combed over a bald spot on the top of his large head, waited in front of the door to Rudy's room.

"You're a week behind on your rent," he said lazily. "If you don't pay me this afternoon, I'll have to kick you out." He shrugged.

Rudy's fists flinched at his side. "You'll have your money in an hour," he answered shortly.

"Muy Bueno. I'll be waiting for you."

In twenty minutes, Rudy had loaded the shotgun and the rest of his belongings into the cab of his truck. He drove past the motel's office without stopping and continued down the hill to the road out of town.

The two women were crossing the street. Rudy stomped his foot down on the accelerator. They had to scamper out of the truck's path to avoid being struck.

He glanced in his rear view mirror.

"They'll remember me," he said aloud. Suddenly his head began to ache.

"Bitches!" he screamed out the open window. "Goddamn bitches!"

September 30

Rudy walked out of Johnny Reb's, a long, ramshackle building with a neon sign that flickered irregularly in the twilight. It was one of those places that fathers warn their sons to avoid. A Santa Ana wind swept over the cars that jammed Harbor Boulevard. Meanwhile, Latino children rode their homemade skateboards up and down the adjacent sidewalk.

A brown-skinned man leaned under the hood of a well-used Ford station wagon, trying to install the used battery he'd just purchased for ten dollars. Rudy's pick-up was parked next to him. For a moment, he sat in the cab and watched the man fumble with his crescent wrench. Then he started the truck and left the parking lot with a screeching of tires.

Almost as soon as he pulled onto the street, he noticed the police car behind him. He reached down to the burlap sack and pulled the shotgun closer.

The truck was passing through the intersection of Harbor and Garden Grove Boulevards when the police car's red lights began flashing. Rudy pulled the pick-up to the curb.

The cop who approached the driver's side of the cab was in his early twenties.

"Driver's license," he demanded.

As the policeman spoke, a short Vietnamese man emerged from an Asian deli. He stood on the sidewalk and squinted into the passenger side of the cab.

Rudy handed over the license.

"One of your taillights is burnt out." The cop shined his flashlight in Rudy's face. "And your license's expired."

He lowered his right hand until it was touching the shotgun's barrel.

"Get real, man," he replied. "Most of the people in this neighborhood don't even bother to get licenses."

"Don't go anywhere," the policeman said.

As he walked back to the patrol car, Rudy grabbed the shotgun and swung open the noisy cab door. By the time his feet hit the asphalt, the cop was pointing his service revolver at Rudy's chest.

"Drop it!" he shouted.

Rudy raised the shotgun's barrel.

The young man fired five rounds into his heart.

As the echo of the gunfire faded, the deli's owner rushed back inside and returned with a fist full of dollar bills. A recent arrival to California, he assumed the policeman was just as corrupt as the ones in his homeland. And that the shooting he'd just witnessed had something to do with an unpaid bribe.

"Here," he said, holding the money out to the cop as the rush hour traffic slowed to gawk at the bloody tableau. "You take."

The policeman stared at him while folks emptied out of the nearby shops and gathered around Rudy's lifeless body.

"You take," the man insisted again. There were tears running down his face.

November 15

Fall had arrived. Orange and yellow oak leaves drifted through the bright, clear sunlight, pushed along by a breeze from the chaparral-covered hills. The towering trees lined the country road. As John drove through their shadows, a jackrabbit darted in front of the car. To avoid the animal, he jerked the Fiesta's steering wheel to the left—and barely missed a scarlet Camaro coming towards him in the opposite lane.

"That was close!" Amanda exclaimed.

"It could only happen to me," he said. "We take a drive in the country and I almost get killed by a jackrabbit."

He never felt sorry for himself before, she thought. He once was strong and selfless. A husband who was faithful, trustworthy. The betrayal he felt because of the family lie had changed him. The ordeal of the false accusation, the trial and living for months in the County Jail had done its damage, too.

The question now was this: Can the damage be repaired? And if not, she told herself, can I stay in love with this man?

She glanced down at the road map. "We're almost to the mission."

"Good. I'm ready to stretch my legs."

The long, whitewashed building's bell tower and red tile roof came into view around a curve in the road. The unpaved parking lot was empty.

"Folks have been neglecting this route in favor of taking the freeway," said the elderly woman who collected their admissions beneath a columned veranda. "It seems like everyone's in a hurry nowadays. Anyway, you have the place all to yourselves."

Past the table where she sat, a wide gateway led to a garden. Ivy covered its adobe walls. A huge pepper tree stood in the middle of the space. Budding camelias rose from the shadows.

They sat together on a small stone bench.

"Can you ever forgive me for everything I've put you through?" he said, looking into her wide hazel eyes.

She squeezed his hand. "Yes," she said. "I can. Because I love you. But I need to know if you still love me."

"I do," he said. "You mean more to me than any one or anything else in the world."

They embraced then as a finch began to sing among the branches of the ancient tree.

December 1

She'd never been to the unemployment office before. In fact, it was the last place she thought she'd ever visit. She'd worked at the restaurant since high school. And figured she might work there forever. But now the owners were going through a messy divorce and had decided to close the place.

Standing just inside the front door, she didn't know what to do. Lines of people were everywhere, all jumbled together. And the directional signs above their heads made no sense to her.

"It's busy this morning, isn't it?"

Beside her stood a man about her age with neatly trimmed brown hair and a friendly face.

"That's for sure."

"Want me to help you get started?"

Her eyes lit up. "That'd be great."

"My name's John," he said, extending his hand.

"I'm Maggie."

After he'd explained the process and gotten her into the correct line, they went their separate ways. But an hour later, they happened to run into one another again as both left the building.

"Let's get a drink," he said. "To celebrate the impending arrival of your first check."

"Why not? Now that I'm unemployed, I don't have any place I need to be."

There was a dive bar at the end of the block that he seemed to be very familiar with. After they sat in a corner booth, she asked: "How long have you been out of work?"

"Most of the year." He paused. "I was out of circulation for a while."

She wondered what that meant, but decided not to ask. After all, they'd just met.

"Why were you at the unemployment office?" he said.

She told him the story of the job at the restaurant and the owners' divorce as they sat there, sipping their cocktails. He was a good listener. I like this guy, she thought. And he's not wearing a wedding ring.

"Should we get another round?" he said.

She studied his face.

"My place isn't far from here," she said. "Why don't we go there?"

He looked into her eyes.

"I like that idea," he said.

DAN BUSTER'S GOLD

I.

Folks hereabouts have dug the whole countryside full of holes looking for Dan Buster's gold. Early in the morning or near sunset, you can look across the fields in the half-light and you would swear there had been half the U.S. Army at work on the valley, if you didn't know better. Even the road is getting filled with trenches. It's worse near the edge of town, where the nine and ten-year-olds already tired of toting their shovels stop in their tracks and start digging. Just last week, I was driving my brand new Model T down the steep ridge on the Fourth Crossing side of the valley. I noticed a dark shape across the bottom. I thought to myself, "That's one hell of a shadow, considering the sun's shining in my face across Farner's fallow field", so I stopped. Sure enough, it was a ditch. Biggest one I had seen in years. Must have been some awful husky youngsters working all night to dig that one. When I told Evans, he didn't seem too concerned, which was what I expected.

"It's probably some of those Mexicans that have been moving up here to work in the vineyards. They haven't been around long enough to know the rules," he said, leaning against the jailhouse's timbered wall. Lazily, he raised his arm and tossed a dart at the board. Missed the bulls eye by a foot, at least. Evans isn't much of a dart player.

"Well," I said, "as sheriff, you had better make sure they learn the rules awful quick. Someone could break their neck driving into that thing after the sun goes down, and I don't need business that bad. Broken necks aren't worth their trouble, anyway."

"All right, Doc, all right," he said, tossing another dart. This time, he missed the entire board. "I'll send some of the boys over to Larson's for shovels and we'll have it filled back up by sunset."

That made sense. One way or another, Darcy Larson's always benefiting from this mess. Same as his father did. If any strangers wander into the general store, you can wager your last dollar they will be rushing out fifteen minutes later with a shovel in each hand and the story of the gold ringing in their ears—only now, it's not forty-five thousand dollars in gold that Buster buried but one-hundred and forty-five thousand. The same thing happens with the young ones. Any time a boy runs back home from an errand in town and starts saving his money like he has heard of a bargain on Salvation, then Larson's got him. And the boy will keep buying shovels from one Larson or another until the day he dies. By then, his son and his son's son will be regular shovel buyers. Dan Buster may be lying under a patch of weeds in the pauper's corner of the old cemetery, but he has done as much to feed the Larsons the past fifty-seven years as planting season has. I don't see any sign that things will ever change, either.

Oh, some years it seems the frenzy over the gold's finally going to tap itself out. The young men start laughing at the story and tell their fathers the fortune was found twenty years ago. But then another Republican gets himself elected President and times turn bad again. Those who try to scratch out a living on the land go broke and put their plows and livestock up for auction--and Larson begins selling shovels like THEY'RE made of gold. After the '07 Panic, the railroad even cancelled the Sheep Ranch stop. "It ain't worth our while anymore," the railroad man said. There were so many folks out digging that half the sheep never got sheared that season.

The thing is, no one doubts that Buster once buried the gold. Larson likes to tell the tale more than anyone else, of course; it's helping him to make a good living without raising any blisters. And because most of the older townspeople are sons and daughters of

Forty-Niners, it's not surprising they have stayed stirred up for all these years, or that the mania over the gold has been passed along to their children and their children's children. The pioneers said farewell to family and loved ones they would never see again and left behind most of what they owned in the world to cross the Mississippi River, trek across the unforgiving deserts and scale the mile-high mountains. Some of them lost even more before they arrived in California; the graves of the infirm, babies and old folks marked the routes they had taken. Then most of those who survived the journey didn't strike enough to cover the cost of the mining equipment they sold their wagons and horses and mules to buy. So they gave up their dreams of riches and, instead, became shopkeepers and shepherds, planted fruit trees and vineyards or got hired on as ranch hands. The sons and daughters, grandsons and granddaughters and great grandsons and great granddaughters know all of this, and realize Dan Buster's gold is their last chance to strike it rich. If one of them ever does find the gold, this town's going to see a celebration that will make the Fourth of July look like a Sunday picnic. It will be a victory celebration: victory over the trail, and California. And over Dan Buster.

II.

It was Ray Clino's father who tested and weighed the gold that blistering August afternoon when Buster led the burros into town. It was strapped onto the animals' backs in old flour sacks.

"Buster was covered with sweat," Ray says, "from stumblin' down Stoney Point, leadin' them animals. It must've taken him all mornin' to load the sacks and get down the hill. When he made the assay office, Daddy wouldn't give him a hand. 'I ain't helpin' no Negro,' he said after Mother looked out and saw Dan Buster liftin' a sack in his arms and looked back at Daddy, standin' behind the counter, countin' the days of the month on the calendar. God, but it was hot, and the flies buzzin' around the black man's head, and him movin' real slow but real steady, droppin' one sack on the counter—PLUNK—and marchin' back out into the heat and the dust to get another. Whole top of the counter was covered when he let the last sack fall."

"The rest of the afternoon, Daddy was busy workin' with the gold. It looked like sand, though there was small nuggests mixed all through it, too. Dan Buster just sat there, in the shadows in the corner of the office, and watched him. Didn't budge an inch from the stool, like he was afraid that if he took his eyes off us to go to the outhouse, or went across the street to the saloon, we'd slip one or two of the sacks under the counter. So he didn't move. Didn't say nothin', either. Only kept his eyes on Daddy.

"Sunset came and Daddy tied the last sack back up and said, "Bout fifty thousand dollars, give or take a dollar or two.' So Dan Buster stood, for the first time all afternoon, and shuffled over to the counter. He reached one of his long brown hands into a sidepocket in his overalls and pulled out a dollar coin and plucked the dollar down on top of one of the sacks. 'Now it's fifty thousand,' he said. Daddy asked: 'What you want done with it?' The miner said: 'I want fifty thousand in gold coins.' 'You must be out of your head,' Daddy said. 'Where are we goin' to get that much in coins out here?'

"So Dan Buster looked down at the dollar on top of the sack. The sweat was still tricklin' down the side of his face and the flies was still buzzin' around his head. The sun was almost gone, but the heat sure hadn't left. Buster said, 'How much in each sack?' Daddy said, 'Five thousand dollars.' Without another word, Buster picked up a sack and carried it out to the burros. He came back in, grasped another and took that one outside. When he came in for a third sack, Daddy said, 'What do I get for all this trouble?'

"Dan Buster stopped and looked at Daddy. Stared at him like he was one of the flies; an uppity, down-the-nose look. After a moment, he picked up the dollar where it was still layin' on top of a sack and suddenly flipped it at Daddy's face. He had to raise his hand, quick-like, to snatch it, or it would've hit him in the nose. And that was it. Buster tossed that coin, picked up the rest of the sacks, one by one, carried them out and disappeared into the cloudless twilight leadin' the burros. The next mornin', everyone in town knew Dan Buster was a rich man."

It wasn't long before everyone in town understood why Buster wanted to know how much was in each sack, too. A week later, he again trudged down from his shack near the top of Stoney Point, the first time he had ever come to town two weeks in a row. This time he left the burros behind. He stopped at the office of H.M. Forrest, the only lawyer the town had.

That fact didn't make everyone happy. Forrest was an Abolitionist. Rumor was he had even made a few speeches on the subject before he came West. A short, fat, balding man, he always wore the same faded red vest, but made sure the vest was clean and pressed, the way he kept his business neat and honest. That was his saving grace. Even the Southerners in town got used to him, because even they couldn't argue against his reputation as a fair man.

Buster must have overheard the whispers about the Abolitionism, despite his hermit-like existence. At any rate, he walked into Forrest's office and dropped five thousand dollars in gold, still in a flour sack, on the lawyer's battered oak desk. "I want you to buy my family," he told the tiny, stunned figure who sat before him.

A runaway slave, Buster's wife and three children were still down South, somewhere in Louisiana or Mississippi; no one could ever remember which. Buster must have figured that, if he wanted to see his family again, Forrest offered his only hope. The last time the miner saw them was the night he fled the plantation, a night filled with countless miles of wandering and re-wandering through stagnated bayous, alligators, water moccasins—and a half dozen hounds that hadn't let a slave get away from them yet. Finally the sun rose and Buster found himself lying among a bunch of crushed reeds on an island in the middle of the Mississippi River he had never seen before and couldn't remember reaching. That was what saved him, because the plantation owner and the dog handler never even considered searching the island; the possibility that the runaway could have somehow reached it in the dark was too unbelievable.

After he had heard Buster's request, Forrest agreed on the spot to serve as his agent. He drew up a contract, read it out loud to the semi-literate miner and had Buster put his mark to it. Only thing was, Forrest turned out to be a lot less honest than everyone had believed. Or maybe the sight of five thousand dollars in gold forced him to take a quick inventory of his principles.

Just after sundown that evening, Ike Clino and Ned Henry, who built the town's livery stable, noticed the little fat man moving about in his office. Curious, they went around to the back alley and caught Forrest as he finished dropping the last of his belongings into his buggy.

"Hey, Forrest," Henry shouted. "Where you goin' in such a hurry?"

Forrest started, and for the only time since he had arrived in the town, he was at a loss for words.

Ray Clino, just a boy at the time, had been sweeping out Forrest's office when Buster arrived. He rushed home afterwards and told his father everything.

"Gonna run off with the Negro's money, huh?" Ike said, smiling and nudging Henry with his elbow. "I guess he ain't as big a no-good Yankee as we thought." The pair guffawed. Then Ike turned to the lawyer again, who was standing motionless on the other side of the horse, watching them somberly.

"Go on," Clino told him lowly. "Get the hell outta here."

No one told Dan Buster. They waited. Six weeks passed and the miner finally came down the hill again and headed for Forrest's office. He tried the padlocked door and peered through the window. It was then that he must have grasped what had happened. He turned in the street and walked back up the hill.

Buster didn't approach the vacant office again for almost five years. Late in '59, a dog-eared envelope with a year-old postmark came for him. It contained an anonymous note with a scrawl which read simply: "Family died in smallpox epidemic." Buster limped away from the post office, worn-out and well past middle age, the note hanging loosely from his hand, weaving in the breeze. He stopped before Forrest's former office and stood there, alone, for ten minutes or so. Then he bent slowly, chose a stone and sent it sailing at the door. By the time it bounced off the splintered and weather-beaten wood, he had let the scrap of paper fall and was on his way back up the hill.

Buster never did use most of the remaining forty-five thousand for anything. Anything anyone took notice of, at any rate. He continued living the life of a recluse and unsuccessful miner, sleeping in his dilapidated one-room shack and going into the hills every day, leading the burros that had become half-blind from age. It began dawning on folks that Dan Buster didn't plan to ever spend the treasure.

One morning in the general store, Darcy Larson's father came right out and asked him: "What you goin' to do with all that gold?"

Buster looked up from the box of cheap vittles he had just purchased.

"You been wantin' to ask me that for a long time, haven't you?" he said.

"What you goin' to do with it?" Larson asked again.

"I took that gold out of the ground with these hands," the miner answered quietly, deliberately, while he stared at Larson. "I put it back in the ground with these same hands."

"Why don't you leave it to me?" Larson asked. "You've got no kin hereabouts. All the years you've been coming into the store, I've treated you right." He paused. "If you try and get it to someone down South," he said, "it'll disappear quicker than the first five thousand did."

Buster stiffened, but his voice was still calm when he spoke again. "You don't need my gold," he said. "You got the store. You got money. I buried that gold. Ain't nobody ever gonna find it." Then he smiled smugly. "There it's gonna stay," he said. "There it's gonna stay where it'll never do no white man no good."

III.

There were other white men a lot more determined than Darcy Larson's father to get the buried treasure, though. The story had been retold so many times that it had gotten all around the Mother Lode country. What happened was probably inevitable. The Sierra foothills were full of rough, unlucky men, searching for a pot of gold at the end of the rainbow which they rarely found. Three of those men figured Dan Buster's gold was at the end of their rainbow.

They rode in late on a cloudy afternoon in January of '61, three months before the Rebels fired on Fort Sumter. Right off, the trio started asking about Dan Buster. But no one in the saloon would tell the strangers anything, including Ike Clino. When the men tried to quiz him about the old miner's whereabouts, he scowled. "You think we'd let a black man live in the same county with us?" he answered. The rest simply refused to talk to them.

Finally the strangers found Dean Keeley, sitting by himself on the ground in the alley at the back of the saloon, drinking from a bottle of rotgut whiskey. He was a miner, too. But he did so poorly that he returned to Arkansas two years later. The strangers offered Keeley five dollars to tell them how to find Buster's shack. He told them—and for weeks afterwards, stumbled drunkenly about town, stopping anyone he met and pleading with them to forgive him. He also tried to hang himself--and failed at that, too.

When the strangers finished talking to Keeley, they glanced at one another and went back into the saloon and drank silently among themselves until sunset. Then they climbed back on their horses and rode up the hill towards the shack.

As soon as they left, the regulars inside the saloon started getting riled up. Clino climbed on top of the bar and shouted: "How in hell are we goin' to ever get our hands on that gold if those three bastards make Buster tell them where it's at?" The men agreed more enthusiastically with each drink. An hour and a half later, Clino was at their head and they, carrying torches and armed with anything they could lay their hands on, followed him up the winding trail that led to the shack.

They met the returning horsemen on a bend in the path.

"There they are!" Clino shouted. "Pull 'em down!"

The strangers charged straight into the midst of the mob—and the mob was drunk enough to let the first two make it through. But Willie Sende—who got blown to pieces fighting for the Confederate side three and a half years later at Cold Harbor--used a shovel to knock the third one down, hitting him square in the face. They picked him up and held on to the limp figure while Clino told them, "Let's see what he's done to the Negro!", and they marched on to the shack.

Dan Buster lay in the dust at the door, bent at the waist and motionless; the strangers had beaten him nearly to death. Clino tried to ask if he told where the gold was, but he was unconscious. So Clino turned to the stranger and asked him, but he was unconscious, too. They left Jay Johnston, the town's doctor at the time, with Buster and dragged their captive a short distance down the hill to a massive birch tree by the side of the trail. The stranger had not come to yet. They took turns shaking and slapping him. But he wouldn't open his eyes. Finally Clino made them stop.

"Can't you see he's fakin'?" he asked them. "Let's string him up and see how good he is at fakin' that!"

The town didn't have a sheriff in those days, so there was no one to stop them. They fashioned a noose, threw it over one of the birch's limbs and lynched him. The stranger hung there, stiff as ever, until Clino figured he must really be dead now and had someone cut the body down.

By this time, it was almost midnight, and someone said, "What if Buster's dead, too?" They trampled back up the hill then, torches blazing in the still, frosted winter air, and stomped into the shack.

Buster lay on his cot, bandaged up in rags Doc Johnston found in the room. As the men crowded around the heaving black body, Doc warned them: "He's not long to go, boys."

"Can he hear us?" Clino asked. "Can he talk?"

"If he can," Doc said, "his next words could be his last."

Clino kneeled at the old man's side.

"Did you tell 'em, Dan?" he said, loudly and quickly.

Dan Buster smiled at the faces in the silent, smoky room.

"No," he hissed. Then he died.

IV.

Three or four of the younger men tore away part of the shack's walls the next morning, but most had the decency to wait two days for the funeral. Everyone knew what would happen the minute the body was laid to rest. Larson's father had been out in front of the store all that morning, holding a shovel over his head and shouting.

"Come on now, you don't want to be left out, do yah?" he told the growing crowd. "There's forty-five thousand in gold buried under that shack, but you need a shovel to get to it!"

They certainly were buying shovels, too—dozens of shovels. They came from as far as Ridgecrest and Sutton, wagons piled high with their families and the supplies they would need for an overnight stay, since they figured that was all the time it would take. "After all," they said, "how well could a man his age hide all those sacks?" And all the while, Larson stood there in the dim sunlight and bitter cold and shouted what they wanted to hear.

"It's all there, must be no more than a hundred feet from the shack," he shouted into the still air. "It's gotta be! Where else could that Negro have put it without somebody noticin'?" Shaking a shovel over his head, he told them: "But you ain't got a chance for it unless you got one of these! And it better be a good one, too, a new shovel that won't bust in your hands in the middle of the rush and a foot above the fortune!" So they kept coming, all morning, pulling their wagons up in front of the general store to listen to Larson's spiel and climbing down and buying shovels for themselves and any sons old enough to help in the digging.

Then Larson ran out of shovels, locked up and joined the rest, sitting in the wagons and on horseback or leaning against the beat-up, unpainted buildings, listening for the word to come. Clino and Henry had paid a boy with one arm to ride down and tell them when Buster had been lowered into his grave by the undertaker and the three old men he found to help him. Clino and the others figured a boy with one arm would be the only person in town they could trust to stop on the way to the shack.

And he did stop, too--rode into the street full of loaded wagons and tense faces, pulled the horse up with one gloved hand, pausing for a second before he shouted:

"He's buried!"

Ten minutes after they reached the shack, there wasn't a shack anymore. They began digging where the shack had been while the women and children sifted through the piles of boards that had been thrown out of the way. They dug all day, even getting the digging organized into shifts because they saw there were too many of them to work in the hole all at once. One group would dig for a half hour or forty-five minutes, then the second shift came on, then the third, and then the first group stepped into the hole again. By sunset, they hadn't found anything. Most left to set up camp for the night. The rest sent Larson back to his store for lanterns.

The next day, they started poking around the clearing surrounding the shack. It wasn't long before the clearing was all dug up. But there was no sign of the gold. By the end of the week, the family men from out of town started packing up. They said they would be back the next chance they got. They kept their word, too.

They—and then their sons and grandsons—have been returning for fifty-seven years. Of course, the townsfolk never stopped the search. Things tapered off the third week after Buster was buried, but that was only because Clino and Henry and the rest had to get back to their businesses, farms and jobs to keep themselves and their families alive—and they had to stay alive to find the gold.

Just last Sunday, Ray and I took a drive in the Model T up to where Buster's shack used to stand. All the way there, we saw folks shoveling away at the sides of the hills. They mostly leave the site of the shack alone, since it has been searched through so many times.

The crater that was dug fifty-seven years ago is still there: filled with truck now, but plenty wide. You can look at it and imagine how deep it must have been once.

"You think anyone will ever find it?" Ray said, spitting into the hole.

"No," I answered. "I think Dan Buster is laughing in his grave." I stared at Ray a moment. "Did it ever occur to you," I said, "that Buster might have told those three men where he buried the gold?"

Ray turned to me. "No," he answered quickly. "He wouldn't have done that." He paused and blinked at the scarred landscape that surrounded us. "Buster just knew how to hide things, goddamn him!" he added angrily, bitterly.

"Yes," I agreed, looking out across the pitted hills and the valley below and the folks busy burrowing here and there. "He sure as hell did."

POEMS

THE RAVENS

One afternoon, pick-up trucks
With license plates from
Iowa and Missouri
And South Carolina
And bright red bumper stickers
Urging other motorists to
"Lock Her Up!"
Pulled up before the
Old white house at the end
Of the unpaved desert road.
The Marines soon filled the
Pair of plastic trash containers
They found behind the house
And set them out front
Without bothering to
Push the lids down tight.

That night, a big wind came along
And blew the trash far and wide,
Filling the darkness
Like an invasion of pint-size ghosts.
When the sun rose over the barren hills,
Wrappers from Del Taco and Burger King
Mingled with instructions on
Interrogating prisoners of war and
Letters from the Veterans Administration,
All impaled on the gray chollas' needles
For as far as the eye could see.

Not long after that,
A pair of ravens arrived
Eager to eat whatever was left
Slathered on the fast food wrappers.
When they finished,
The loud black birds
Filled their beaks with
Discarded love letters
From lonesome sweethearts and wives
And flew together
To the nest they'd begun building
In the rocky hillside
Above the valley floor.

ACID REFLUX BLUES

I've scarfed up haute cuisine
At Guy Savoy on the banks of the Seine,
Spent long evenings at Aimo and Nadia's
Chowin' down on sirloin of veal to die for
Yes, I've drank my fill of Forestville Pinot
And Williamette Valley's finest vino
Know my way around Kentucky's distilleries
Have explored Old Vermont's finest breweries
Anthony Bourdain got nothin' on me
But my doctor says it all has to cease.

No more whisky, no more wine or beer
No more fatty meats--farewell, cheer!
Desserts and chocolate are at an end
Spicy Mexican burrito? No mas, my friend
Now it's watermelon
I'm havin' in my dwellin'
Hummus and celery stalks
Instead of rich tomato sauce
Carrot sticks, peanut butter
In place of pie made by my grandmother.

Walkin' down my street one day,
I heard a little blonde girl along the way
Singin' a song to chase the blues away.
"Here comes the sun," she crooned
Fillin' the air with that Beatles tune
All I could think was: Screw the sun today!
Let me have a brisket sandwich and soon
Bring on fried chicken, come what may
Or a nice marbled ribeye steak
Or anything else I crave
But can no longer put away.

That's when my baby
Whispered in my ear:
"How about a slice of avocado toast
Covered with a runny egg, my dear?"
After I'd eaten every bite,
She slipped out of her sexy shift,
Took my hand and led me to bed
And in no time I didn't give a damn
About those motherfriggin'
Acid Redux Blues.

BOSTON MOUNTAINS FLASHBACK

Covey of quail, scratching at sand
Beneath a blooming Joshua tree
Reminds me of roosters and hens
Scattered about an Arkansas
Farmyard, hunting for the corn my
Grandmother had tossed to them.

"Wonder who owns the farm now,"
My brother said a while back.
I shrugged and shook my head
Since I haven't visited the
Boston Mountains in thirty-three years.
From where I sat on the front porch,
The desert stretched to the south, towards
The barren valley and the
Eternal silhouette of hills beyond.

THE OLDEST LIVING THING ON EARTH

One-hundred and seventeen centuries--
That's how long it's hunkered down
In the depths of the Mojave
Surrounded by nothing
Except desolation
And other creosote bushes.
Inch-by-inch, decade after decade,
Its roots dig deeper
Into the desert's infertile soil,
Seeking their own path
Through the sand and rock
Finding water and refuge from
The bad news all around them.
They've missed the
Extinction of the saber-toothed cats,
Know nothing of the
Disappearance of ancient lakes
Or exploitation of the valleys and
Mountains around them
By miners, ranchers, outlaws
And off-roaders
Never heard of
The decimation of the native peoples
Or internment of the nation's
Japanese-American citizens.
Yes, I envy the creosote roots
Able to hide away, seek shelter
For the last
One-hundred and seventeen centuries
While I toss and turn in my bed
Hoping against hope that I'll
Fall asleep and forget
What the creosote roots
Have never known.

RYLAND ROAD

His life was filled with troubles
He needed someone to settle him down
That's when she caught his eye
Among the karaoke bar's cast of clowns

"Let's go someplace special," he said
Soon they were on their way to Ryland Road
She listened till dawn as the handsome stranger
Transfixed her with his tall tales and bull

Just graduated from the junior college
She'd volunteered at a horse rescue ranch
And was waiting for someone to come along
Who could make her dull life special at last

It was six months later when she asked him
To again drive into the hills on Ryland Road
When they arrived at the mine, she said:
"I'm so happy. I'm pregnant with our baby girl"

Taking responsibility was not what he cared for
Something he had no desire to assume--
Besides, he had another woman now
And freedom to burn

The open shaft loomed behind her
When he was a boy, the kids all believed
The hole was so deep it reached down
To the Inferno that Dante had conceived

She may be a God-fearing woman
But he abruptly decided then and there
That sending her to meet the devil
Was the way to wipe away his cares

"I'm so happy about the baby," he lied
As he wrapped her tightly in his arms
But before she knew what was happening
He threw her into the darkness and fatal harm

In no time the county detectives
Got to the bottom of this missing person case
As well as to the bottom of the mine shaft
And the saddest scene they'd ever faced

Now he's waiting for his turn on death row
And she's buried in the cemetery in town
But at midnight the sound of her weeping
Follows the curves of Ryland Road

Her sorrow haunts the arroyos and the ridges
Rises to touch the Belt of Orion
And finally rattles the gates
Of heaven itself

EPIPHANY FOR ME

White post-op lights
   Filled my cloudy eyes
      Left groggy and hung over
         By the general anesthesia
         And fearing what the
            Surgeon found
               I blinked and there
               She was.

ONE-HUNDRED AND SEVEN DEGREES

One-hundred and seven degrees
Reveals the thermometer on the garden wall
I stare through the picture window's glass
Like a child or a visitor from another world.
Here rattlesnakes mate beside a cholla cactus
And there, at the top of a Joshua Tree,
A pair of roadrunners roost and clack.
Strangeness and wonder are everywhere
At one-hundred and seven degrees.

PANDEMIC TWILIGHT

Smoke from the
Brush fire down below
Fills up the Morongo Basin
Hides the Joshua Trees
And the jackrabbits
Blocks out the sky
Gives us a Martian sunset
Perfect twilight
For a pandemic.

THE LADY FROM UTAH

There lived a lady from Utah
Who'd seen hardship all her days
Worked long hours at Walmart
To pay for her father's whisky

Then she fell in love with Freddie Silva
A foreman at the meat packing plant
Soon she knew a baby was on the way
And made plans for her wedding day

Her angry father to his daughter came
"Stop seein' that Mexican!" he screamed
"Even if you load your shotgun," she said
"I will not forsake Freddie Silva"

She found one of her seven sisters
To carry the tidings to her betrothed
"Tell him I'll love him all my life
And tell him to find another wife."

Her drunk father waited for her
As she drove by on the way to work
Fired three shells into the windshield
And used the fourth to kill himself

When the graveside service ended
Her sisters wandered away in a daze
While Freddie Silva whispered
"Aqui estoy mi amor"

There lived a lady from Utah
Who'd seen hardship all her days
Worked long hours at Walmart
And is buried with her baby

ETERNAL AS THE SCARLET SKY

One lazy desert afternoon
The old man fell asleep
To dream once again
Of a day fifty years before.
Cantina tequila shots
Lobster fresh off the grill
San Felipe sunset tides
And a midnight spent
With someone else's wife.
At twilight he awoke
And the green eyes
Of his star-crossed love
Still lingered in his mind
Eternal as the scarlet sky.

ONCE AGAIN

Careful and quiet
The coyotes crept
Through the
Midnight gloom
Beneath a
Crescent moon
Waiting until
The time was right
To sing their
Freedom tune
Their muzzles
Pointed skyward
Their voices
Filled the dark
Suddenly the
Void above us all
Had never felt
Less stark
Then the
Howling stopped
As quickly as
It started
And the desert
Felt too lonely
Once again.

JESUS WALKS THE EARTH

The sky is crying
Its tears pooling
On the garden patio
While I stare at the front page photo:
The young man and his little girl
Huddled together on the muddy shore
Both face down in the dirty water
Both soaking wet, still and departed.
The sky is crying
I step into the
Downpour
Feel the drops
Roll down my face
Until they mingle
With my tears.

Photo by Caylie Phillips

Michael G. Vail

Michael G. Vail is a novelist, short story author and poet. High Desert Elegy is his second book. The Salvation of San Juan Cajon, his novel about the desperate struggle to construct a new high school in a poverty-stricken urban community, was published in 2018. A California native, Mr. Vail divides his time between San Clemente and a former homestead cabin in the Mojave Desert.

Made in the USA
Coppell, TX
28 April 2021

54676413R00104